Stories, sayings, and scriptures to Encourage and Inspire

"拥抱·爱"系列双语典藏读物

hugs™

for
Heroes

勇敢的心

Larry Keefauver
Leann Weiss   著

杜建礼 译

安徽科学技术出版社

HOWARD
PUBLISHING CO.

[皖] 版贸登记号:1208543

图书在版编目(CIP)数据

拥抱·爱. 勇敢的心:英汉对照/(美)基福弗(Keefauver, L.)著;杜建礼译.—合肥:安徽科学技术出版社,2009.1
ISBN 978-7-5337-4264-5

Ⅰ.拥… Ⅱ.①基…②杜… Ⅲ.①英语-汉语-对照读物②故事-作品集-美国-现代 Ⅳ.H319.4:Ⅰ

中国版本图书馆 CIP 数据核字(2008)第 198277 号

拥抱·爱. 勇敢的心:英汉对照

(美)基福弗(Keefauver, L.) 著 杜建礼 译

出　版　人:黄和平
责任编辑:付　莉
封面设计:朱　婧
出版发行:安徽科学技术出版社(合肥市政务文化新区圣泉路 1118 号
　　　　　出版传媒广场,邮编:230071)
电　　话:(0551)3533330
网　　址:www.ahstp.net
E - mail: yougoubu@sina.com
经　　销:新华书店
排　　版:安徽事达科技贸易有限公司
印　　刷:安徽江淮印务有限责任公司
开　　本:787×1240　1/32
印　　张:6.75
字　　数:85 千
版　　次:2009 年 1 月第 1 版　2009 年 1 月第 1 次印刷
印　　数:6 000
定　　价:16.00 元

(本书如有印装质量问题,影响阅读,请向本社市场营销部调换)

给爱一个归宿
——出版者的话

身体语言是人与人之间最重要的沟通方式,而身体失语已让我们失去了很多明媚的"春天",为什么不可以给爱一个形式?现在就转身,给你爱的人一个发自内心的拥抱,你会发现,生活如此美好!

肢体的拥抱是爱的诠释,心灵的拥抱则是情感的沟通,彰显人类的乐观坚强、果敢执著与大爱无疆。也许,您对家人、朋友满怀缱绻深情却羞于表达,那就送他一本《拥抱·爱》吧。一本书,七个关于真爱的故事;一本书,一份荡涤尘埃的"心灵七日斋"。一个个叩人心扉的真实故事,一句句震撼心灵的随笔感悟,从普通人尘封许久的灵魂深处走出来,在洒满大爱阳光的温情宇宙中尽情抒写人性的光辉!

"拥抱·爱"(Hugs)系列双语典藏读物是"心灵鸡汤"的姊妹篇,安徽科学技术出版社与美国出版巨头西蒙舒斯特携手倾力打造,旨在把这套深得美国读者青睐的畅销书作为一道饕餮大餐,奉献给中国的读者朋友们。

每本书附赠CD光盘一张,纯正美语配乐朗诵,让您在天籁之音中欣赏精妙美文,学习地道发音。

世界上最遥远的距离,不是树枝无法相依,而是相互凝望的星星却没有交会的轨迹。

"拥抱·爱"系列双语典藏读物,助您倾吐真情、启迪心智、激扬人生!

一本好书一生财富,今天你拥抱了吗?

A SPECIAL GIFT FOR

_____

WITH LOVE,

_____

_____

DATE

Contents

Heroes
Take
Risks

Chapter

1

1

英雄勇于冒险

I am with you, and I am mighty to save. I command My angels concerning you—guarding you in all your ways. Because you love Me, I'll rescue and protect you.

我和你在一起，而且我有能力来拯救你。我命令我的天使关照你——随时在你的人生道路上保护你，因为你爱着我，因此我要拯救并保护你。

When you call upon Me, I will answer. I'll
be with you in trouble.   I will deliver and
honor you. I will satisfy you with long life,
showing you My salvation.

RESCUING YOU,
YOUR SAVIOR AND STRONGHOLD
—from Zephaniah 3:17; Psalm 91:11, 14–16

你若求告我,我就应允你,你在急难中,我要
与你同在。我要搭救你,使你尊贵,我要使你
足享长寿,将我的救恩显明给你。

拯救你
救世主和众神之地
——摘自:《西番雅》3:17;《诗篇》91:11,14-16

What are heroes thinking when they bravely risk all for someone in danger? They're thinking of the grave risk the person faces if they don't act. What are heroes not thinking when they perform that heroic deed? The possible risk to themselves.

That's not to say heroes act without awareness. It's just that in the minds of heroes, the possible risk to themselves doesn't measure up to the certain dire consequences for someone else if they don't act.

Not every risk heroes

accept is monumental or life-threatening.
Not everyone who risks is recognized as a
hero, but they are. Risking a job to defend the
unpopular truth, risking our vision of the future
to accommodate the needs of a sick family
member, risking our reputation by admitting a
mistake someone else was blamed for—
these are the risks that mark the lives of
everyday heroes.

What difficult decision are you
facing today? What would you risk
by doing the right thing?
Embrace the risk. Be a hero.

当英雄们奋不顾身地替身处险境的人冒

险的时候,他们在想些什么呢? 英雄们想的是,如果他

们不出手,身陷险境的人将面临巨大的危险。那么,当英

雄们做出自己英勇壮举时,没有想到的事情是什么呢? 是

自身潜在的危险。

然而这并不是说英雄们做事就没有头脑。恰恰

是在英雄们的意识里有这样的想法;如果他们

不挺身而出的话,把自身的潜在危险与确

定发生在别人身上的可怕后果相衡

量,那简直是微不足道的。

并不是英雄们所受

到的每一

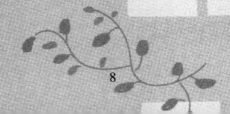

个危险都会被世人记住或者是危及生命的。并不是所有勇于冒险的人都被人称为英雄,然而他们就是英雄。勇于冒险来承担一项工作以此来捍卫证明不为大多数人所接受的事实;勇于挑战世俗对未来的看法来满足患病家人的需要;勇于冒险不畏权贵来认同一个别人因而受责的错误——这些都是冒险,这些冒险标志着寻常英雄们的存在。

如今,你正面临着什么艰难的抉择?通过做正确的事情你会冒险做些什么呢?拥抱艰险,做个真正的英雄。

We never know
how high we are
Till we are asked to rise;
And then,if we are
true to plan,
Our statures
touch the skies.

—Emily Dickinson

我们永远都不知道，
自己到底有多高，
直到有人让我们继续上升；
那时候，
如果我们实实在在地好好计划，
必将与天相接，漫步云端。

——艾米莉·迪克森

艾米看到一个十几岁的男孩的身影就站在她的面前——鲨鱼的嘴里。

Amy *saw the form of a teenaged boy just feet in front of her—and in the jaws of the shark.*

Race of a Lifetime

★ ★ ★ ★ ★ ★ ★ ★ ★ ★ ★ ★ ★ ★ ★ ★ ★ ★

Amy soaked up the late August sun as she sat atop her lifeguard post at the small public beach. The surf was up, and a solitary surfer worked the waves. Local schools were back in session, so most late-afternoon surfers wouldn't arrive for another hour. She breathed deeply, enjoying the soothing sounds of the ocean and the warm breeze.

Lifeguarding was the ideal job for Amy, who dreamed of becoming a champion swimmer. Her schedule at the beach worked well with her training regimen, and the additional on-duty time in the water helped build her strength and stamina.

As she casually watched the surfer, Amy day-dreamed about her next meet and envisioned herself being the first to cross the finish line. She opened her cooler filled with ice and bottled water and pulled out a cold drink to quench her thirst. Amy took a long, slow gulp, savoring the refreshment, and wiped perspiration from her face with the corner of her beach towel.

Scanning the surf again, Amy became uneasy and shifted in her seat, straining for a clearer view. She saw the surfer's board but no longer saw the young man. "Where is he?" she said aloud as she reached nervously for her binoculars. Searching the water around the empty board, Amy saw nothing but waves.

She jumped up, grabbing the buoy rope and slinging it over her shoulder, and ran into the surf. She swam with long, powerful strokes toward the bobbing surfboard. When she reached her destination, she located the ankle rope and dove down, hoping to find the surfer still linked to his board.

Suddenly something in the murky surf bumped hard

into her. As Amy spun around, horror flooded her right to the bone. The gray object that had hit her was a shark fin. As split seconds took on the feeling of time in slow motion, Amy saw the form of a teenaged boy just feet in front of her—and in the jaws of the shark.

Amy surged to the surface, gasping for air. Then something took over. She gulped down as big a reserve of air as her lungs could hold and dove back toward the shark with ferocity. Terrified but determined to rescue the young man, Amy gathered all the force she could muster and delivered one powerful kick to the shark's snout.

Surprised more than hurt, the shark opened its mouth just long enough for Amy to snatch the suffer and lunge frantically back toward the surface. She draped the boy's body over the buoy and swam furiously toward the shore.

With every kick stroke, Amy mentally braced herself for an attack from behind and fought off panic. She expected razor-sharp teeth to clamp down on her legs, sending shock-waves of searing pain through her body, at any second.

Desperation drove her to swim harder than she ever had in the heat of competition. This race wasn't against other swimmers but against the odds that she and her nearly drowned surfer would survive. The finish line wasn't a painted bar at the bottom of the pool but the safety of shore. Amy gasped for breath and reached deep within herself for the strength to push the dead weight of her victim through the surging tide.

Amy was so focused that the feeling of her foot touching sand startled her. *Why didn't the shark attack?* She wondered as she stood up quickly and dragged the limp surfer through the final twenty-five yards of ocean toward the beach. *He's lifeless,* her thoughts raced. *He could already be dead. Where is the shark?*

Once on the sand, Amy immediately began CPR. Pounding the victim's chest and breathing methodically into his mouth, Amy counted and worked hard. As quickly and surely as the aching pain of fatigue swept through her muscles, a sense of hopelessness invaded her mind as the wet, clammy body under her refused to offer any sign of life.

Still, Amy's adrenaline and dogged determination wouldn't let her give up. Finally, the surfer coughed—at first sporadically and then spasmodically. His whole body shook. Water and vomit gushed out of his mouth. Amy lifted him up to a sitting position and pounded his back, trying to help him cough up the rest of the salt water. He trembled as his shallow gasps grew into deep, wrenching gulps of life-giving air.

Once the victim's airway was clear, Amy laid him back down on the sand to survey his injuries. As she glanced down at his legs, a scream escaped her before she could help it. In her frantic attempt to resuscitate her patient, Amy hadn't noticed the damage done to his lower right leg by the shark's jaws.

The surfer's foot lay separately from his leg, attached only by a solitary ligament. His skin and bone had been severed.He was losing blood fast and was in shock. Amy wrapped her beach towel around his upper calf for a makeshift tourniquet, and the blood stopped gushing. The surfer was still breathing, but she could barely feel his pulse, and he was unconscious.

Amy ran to her lifeguard stand to call for an ambulance. Then she grabbed her ice chest, threw out the excess water,and returned to the victim.   Amy grimaced as she took firm hold of the foot and gave one forceful yank.   The ligament snapped,   and she packed the severed foot in the ice and closed the cooler.

Shuddering with horror at the gruesomeness of her task, Amy heard sirens and turned to see the ambulance approaching.   Paramedics rushed to the scene and checked the victim's vital signs.   They administered oxygen and carried the suffer on a stretcher into the waiting emergency vehicle.   It all happened so quickly that Amy hardly uttered anything but a few bits of vital information to the medical team.

When the ambulance pulled away,   two police officers arrived to check on Amy and gather information for their report. Dazed, exhausted, and overwhelmed, Amy finally allowed herself to react.   She began to tremble, and she sat down quickly, feeling her knees start to give out beneath her. In the aftermath of trauma, tears now flowed freely down her cheeks.

A small band of surfers just arriving at the beach also gathered around as Amy explained to the officers what had happened. Amy wrapped herself in a beach towel loaned to her by one of the surfers and shivered in disbelief as she told of her terrifying encounter with the shark.

When she had given police the information they needed, Amy persuaded them to take her to the hospital to follow up on the shark-attack victim. When they arrived, she rushed into the emergency-room waiting area just as the receptionist was telling other officers that the boy had been rushed to surgery. A team of surgeons was being hastily assembled for the tedious and difficult task of trying to successfully reattach the foot.

Several hours later, the surgery was completed. Now only time would tell whether the operation had been a success. Amy learned that the boy's name was Tom and that he was only sixteen. Throughout his recovery, Amy kept in touch and frequently visited him in the hospital, encouraging him to hope for the best and focus on recovery.

Six weeks later, Amy was honored in a ceremony outside the small city hall of her seaside village. She listened appreciatively as local dignitaries, police, rescue workers, and doctors praised her rescue effort. Amy's courage, quick thinking, and swift action had saved Tom's life and his foot.

Amy's favorite part of the ceremony, however, was when she looked across the parking lot and spotted Tom, who was recovering well and, miraculously, was on his way to regaining full use of his right foot. Their eyes met—surfer and lifeguard, victim and rescuer. Tom's expression spoke a gratitude that only a person who had been given a second chance at life could communicate and that only a hero could understand. Amy could ask for no better reward.

鲨口逃生

在这个小小的公共海滩上，艾米坐在救生员专用的高台上，沐浴着8月底的阳光，海水波涛汹涌，只有一个冲浪者在搏击海浪。当地许多学校都到了开学期，因此大部分傍晚冲浪者不会在接下来的一个小时内到达。她深呼一口气，享受着海洋平静的声音和温暖的微风。

对于艾米来说，她过去就梦想着成为一名游泳冠军，救生对她来说就是理想的工作。在这片海滩上，她的工作日程表与训练安排相得益彰。而且在水里的那些额外工作时间使她的身体更加强健

有力。

　　艾米不经意地看着那个冲浪者。她幻想着下一次运动会，脑海中浮现出自己第一个冲过终点的情景。她打开冰箱，里面满是加满冰的瓶装水，她抽出一瓶冷饮想解解渴。艾米猛喝了一大口顿感神清气爽，再用海滩浴巾的一角擦掉脸上的汗水。

　　艾米再一次扫视了一下海浪，她突然有些不安起来，在座位上来回移动，希望看得更清晰些。她看得到冲浪者的帆板，但是那个年轻人却不见踪影。"他哪儿去了呢？"她一边大声地说着一边紧张地拿起望远镜搜寻着空帆板周围的水域，可看到的除了海浪一无所有。

　　艾米跳起来，迅速抓起浮标绳甩在肩上，冲进浪里。她采用幅度大而有力的自由泳方式游向跃动的帆板。她游到目的地，把绳子系在脚踝上，向水下潜去，希望看到冲浪者仍旧和他的冲浪板连在一起。

　　突然，模糊之中有什么东西向她这边狠狠撞过来。艾米急忙旋

转着躲避,一阵惊恐袭上心头渗入骨髓。撞上她的白色东西竟然是

一条鲨鱼的鳍。那几秒钟时间如同放慢了一般,艾米看到一个十来

岁男孩的身影就站在自己面前——竟然在鲨鱼的嘴里。

艾米浮出水面大口喘气,稍微平息一下。她深吸一口气使肺部

达到最大的承受力,然后朝鲨鱼所在的方向猛游过去。尽管她也害

怕,但是她更坚定要去救这个小伙子。于是,艾米攒足力气用尽全

力,朝着鲨鱼的口鼻部位狠踢了一脚。

鲨鱼与其说是受伤倒不如说是受到了惊吓,把嘴张开了,时间

刚好够让艾米抓住男孩,然后疯了一般地向水面游回去。她把男孩

拖进救生圈慌慌张张地向岸上游。

每游一次,埃米的大脑里就担心自己背后会受到袭击,心里满

是恐慌。她感觉就像刮胡刀一样锋利的牙齿将她的腿咬住一样,每

一秒钟钻心的疼痛都一浪一浪向她袭来。

绝望中,她在这场如火如荼的生命竞赛中,她游得比刚才更拼命了。目标不是要击败别的游泳者而是要赢得危在旦夕的生命,因为这决定着她和那个奄奄一息的男孩会不会幸存。这场比赛的终点不是位于水塘底部色彩斑斓的酒吧,安全到达岸上才算平安无事。艾米气喘吁吁,大口喘气,游到水面以下积蓄力量把这个死沉死沉的受害人拖过汹涌的浪潮。

艾米太专注了以至于脚接触沙地的感觉让她大吃一惊。"为什么刚才鲨鱼没有攻击我们呢?"她疑惑不解地起身,然后拖着软成一团的受害人趟过距离海滩25码的最后一段海域。"他没气了,"她的脑海里疾闪过这个念头。"他可能早就死了。鲨鱼在哪儿呢?"

一到沙滩上艾米就开始抢救这个人。她用手连续按压受害人的胸口,有节奏地对他进行人工呼吸,艾米满怀期望竭尽全力地工作着。很快一种疲惫不堪的痛苦涌遍全身每块肌肉;而当她面前这个满身湿漉漉,冰冷的身体对她所做的努力毫无反应的时候,她大脑里涌上一种万念俱灰的感觉。

艾米坚持不懈地继续努力着,她的顽强意志力不允许她放弃。终于这个人有了反应,开始咳嗽——起先是很久才咳嗽一次,然后就是断断续续地咳嗽。他的全身开始颤动,水和污物开始从嘴里涌出。艾米把他扶起来坐着,然后开始敲打他的后背,想帮助他把胃里残存的海水咳干净。随着小伙子的气息由弱变强,他开始哆嗦起来,同时大口大口地呼吸着供给生命的空气。

伤者的呼吸道刚刚畅通,艾米就让小伙子平躺在沙滩上,开始为他检查受伤情况。她向下瞅了一眼小伙子的腿,不由自主地大声尖叫起来。原来在她发疯似的抢救病人之时,艾米从未注意到原来鲨鱼的巨颚给小伙子的右小腿造成伤害。

这个人的右脚和他的腿断开了,单靠一条韧带连接着。他的皮肤和骨头受伤严重,流血不止,人也吓坏了。艾米把浴巾绑在他的小腿上部代替绷带止血,血很快就止住了。小伙子还在喘气,不过艾米几乎摸不到他的脉搏,他处于昏迷状态。

艾米跑到救生带打电话叫救护车。然后她拍打着自己冰冷的胸部，吐出呛进去的水，又回到小伙子身边。当艾米紧紧地握住那只受伤的脚然后用力一拉时，她的脸上掠过一丝痛苦；韧带断了，她把那只脚用冰裹住然后放进冰箱。

在为自己工作的危险性惊恐未定之时，艾米听见警笛声，转身看到救护车飞驰而至。医护人员下车急冲到现场，开始检查受害者的身体状况。他们给他输氧气，把他抬上担架送进正在等待的救护车。所有的事情发生得太快了，以至于艾米除了向医护队粗略说了一点关键信息外，剩下的几乎都没说 。

救护车开走后，两名警官过来开始询问艾米事情的经过，同时为他们的报告收集相关信息。眩晕、疲惫和不安终于使得艾米自我释放。她开始哆嗦，于是马上坐下来，顿时感到自己的两膝不听使唤失去了知觉。由于受到严重的精神创伤，艾米的泪水肆无忌惮地顺着脸颊流淌下来。

一小群冲浪者刚好来到海滩，当艾米向警官说明刚才发生的事情时，他们也都聚拢过来围观。艾米接过一位冲浪者递过来的浴巾将自己裹起来，当讲述自己与鲨鱼那段恐怖经历时，她颤抖着，自己都不敢相信。

当艾米将警官们需要的信息向他们讲完之后，她说服他们把她带到医院去陪伴那个受到鲨鱼袭击的小伙子。他们一到医院，艾米就不顾一切地冲进急诊室，这时医院的接待员说明了情况：那个男孩早就急送到外科手术室了，一队外科医生正紧急会诊，研究能成功接好那只脚的办法，这是个漫长而艰巨的任务。

几个小时后手术完成了。现在，只有时间能告诉大家这次手术成功与否。艾米了解到男孩名叫汤姆而且只有16岁。在他整个恢复期间，艾米一直同他保持联络并经常到医院探望他，不断鼓励他，让他凡事往好处想。

6周后，在艾米所在的海边村庄的小镇礼堂外举行了一场典礼，她获得了应有的荣誉。当本地的上层人士、警察、救护工作者以及医生们为她所做的救援努力而赞叹不已时，她感激地聆听着人们对她的赞扬。艾米的勇气、机智灵活和快速反应挽救了汤姆的脚和生命。

典礼上最让艾米高兴的是，当目光掠过停车场时，她认出了汤姆。他恢复得很好，而且，他的右脚正奇迹般地逐渐完全康复。他们的目光相遇——冲浪者与救生员——受伤者与救援者。汤姆的表情满是感激：这是被赋予了第二次生命的人才能有的感情和作为一名英雄才能明白的真真切切的感情。艾米得到了最好的回报。

Heroes
Are
Compassionate

Chapter
2

②

英雄善良仁爱

With everlasting kindness, I'm compassionate and loving toward you. Let me enlighten the eyes of your heart so you'll know the hope I've destined for you. Don't just think about yourself; be considerate of others.

我满怀永恒的善良,对你充满仁慈,并且始终不渝地爱着你。让我为你点亮你心灵深处的明灯,这样你就会看到我给你的希望与信念。别只是想着自己,为他人多考虑一些吧。

Show mercy and compassion to one another. As you continue to commit everything you do to Me, I'll make you successful.

ROMPASSIONATELY,
YOUR GOD OF ALL COMFORT
—from Isaiah 54:8; Ephesians 1:18–9;
Philippians 2:3–4; Zechariah 7:9; Proverbs 16:3

向你身边的每个人表达你对他们的同情与仁慈之心。如果你坚持不懈地对我实行你所做的一切,我就会让你获得成功。

仁慈的,
能抚慰你内心的上帝
——摘自:《以赛亚书》54:8;《以弗所书》1:18–19;
《腓力比书》2:3–4;《撒迦利亚》7:9;《箴言》16:3

Heroes possess a wellspring of compassion, and they demonstrate that compassion through heroic actions and words.

With heroic compassion, Abraham Lincoln penned the Gettysburg address. Florence Nightingale dressed wounds in the Crimea. Martin Luther King Jr. voiced a dream of liberty for the oppressed.

Compassion motivates people to perform heroic acts of bravery, kindness, and generosity. It's the force that moves rescuers to brave the worst of storms to reach helpless victims and relief workers to travel to Third-World countries to provide relief after tragedy.

Compassion also is manifested in quieter but no less heroic ways. Because they feel the pain of others, heroes cry...heroes pray... heroes overcome obstacles...and heroes persevere.

Heroic compassion makes a difference in the lives of others. Perhaps someone near you is hurting or in need. Perhaps that person's wounds can be healed, his hurts soothed, her life changed by a compassionate word or act from a hero like you.

英雄拥有慈悲的源泉，他们通过英勇行

为和话语来表明他们的仁慈之心。

正是有了英雄般的仁慈之心，亚伯拉罕·林肯才写

成了葛底斯堡演说；弗罗伦斯·南丁格尔才会在克里米亚

半岛照料伤员穿衣；马丁·路德·金才会高唱出在压迫中

寻求自由的梦想。

仁慈促使人们做出英雄的事迹，包括勇敢义

举、善良行为和慷慨之举。它就是一种力量，这

一力量使得救援者勇于冒着暴风雨的残

酷来到无助的受难者身边；这一力

量还促使从事慈善和救援工

作的人员远涉第三

世界国家，

为

那里受到悲惨遭遇的人们提供慰藉。

温和的方式也会表现出仁慈之心，而且绝不会比英勇的方式表现得差。因为他们都感受着别人的痛苦，所以英雄们会流泪，英雄会为他人祈祷……英雄勇于排除万难……而且英雄坚持不懈。

英雄的仁慈之心会给他人的人生带来意外的惊喜。也许，你身边的人现在正承受伤害，或者需要别人的帮助;也许,通过像你一样的英雄般人物的一句善意话语或者一个善意举动，某个人的伤就会得到治愈，他的伤痛就会被抚平,她的人生会因此而改变。

God is a Specialist
at making something
useful and beautiful
out of something
broken and confused.

—Charles R. Swindoll

上帝不是一个搞破坏和制造混乱的专家；相反，她是一个创造有用及美好事物的行家。

——查尔斯·阿·斯温达尔

他不清楚是药物作用还是心脏手
术的原因，然而某些东西确确实
实地影响了他的心灵。

He *didn't know if it
had been the medicine
or the angioplasty,
but something had
def initely affected
his heart.*

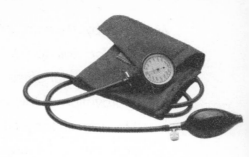

The Heart of a Hero

★ ★ ★ ★ ★ ★ ★ ★ ★ ★ ★ ★ ★ ★ ★ ★ ★ ★ ★

The gray, wintry weather outside seemed to penetrate the window of the semiprivate hospital room through half-pulled shades. Jack felt as gloomy as the view. Severe chest pains had brought him to the emergency room the evening before, and now he lay in bed in the hospital's coronary care unit.

*Angioplasty…me?…this can't be…*Jack struggled to comprehend his situation. Although medication dulled his pain to a vague discomfort, the drugs failed to relieve the nagging irritation that his schedule, usually crammed with business meetings, was now out of his control. *Today is*

Monday...by Thursday morning I have to be on a plane headed for Chicago to put out a corporate fire in our Midwest regional office. He grimaced, teeth clenched, at the aggravation of this unscheduled event.

He had already called the office and instructed his assistant not to let anyone know about his emergency. He wanted no visitors, no calls, no flowers or cards—no sympathy. All Jack wanted was to recover quickly so he could get back to his own agenda. He shut his eyes to block out the two other people in the room. "I can't believe there were no private rooms available," he grumblecd to himself.

But his restlessness wouldn't let his eyes remain closed. His gaze skipped around the room and landed on his roommate. The elderly man rarely stirred as he gasped to get air through the oxygen mask tethered to his face. He seemed quite ill, and his diminutive wife looked weary as she laced her bony fingers affectionately with his.

Something about the old couple struck him hard. The tenderness and love they felt for one another was unmistakable. There was a new, strange sensation in

Jack's malfunctioning heart. All of his success, money, and reputation could never afford him what this modest little couple so obviously had.

Jack had never had time for a wife or family. His college education had launched him from business school into a hectic career that consumed his time and emotions. He wondered, when the end of his life came, would anyone look at him with such longing and concern? Would anyone stay by his side, hold his hand, pray for his recovery, and mourn his loss? If his heart procedure turned out badly—and he would be a fool not to at least consider that possibility—he knew he would die an incredibly poor man.

Suddenly he could hardly bear that thought. It made him uncomfortable. It made him grumpy. He pushed the thought away and tried to distract his mind with business priorities.But his gaze and his thoughts turned again to the man in the next bed and the woman beside him. This time they reminded him of his own aging parents two thousand miles away. A wave of nostalgia and regret flooded him as he reflected on how little time he had spent with them over the years and how lonely they must be.

Jack felt he needed to speak to the woman across the room. "How's your husband, Emma?"

The elderly woman looked up, startled. "I heard the nurse call you Emma," he explained, realizing for the first time that they were more a part of his world than he was of theirs.

The answer satisfied her, and she looked back toward her husband, sadly. "Not good," she replied. "John isn't well. He had a pacemaker put in, but he's not responding well. I'm so worried," she admitted, then dissolved into silent tears.

While Jack tried to decide what he could say to comfort Emma, orderlies came with a gurney to wheel him away for his procedure. "See you later," he said weakly to Emma. Jack rarely prayed these days, but this was certainly the time to reach back and pull up some spiritual strength both for himself and for an elderly couple all alone. "I'll pray for you both," Jack promised as he was wheeled out the door.

As they passed into the hallway, Jack studied the name below his own posted outside the room. Vanderhassen. An unusual name, he thought. Vanderhassen. Vanderhassen. Suddenly it felt important to remember that name.

God, please bless Emma and John Vanderhassen, Jack prayed silently as he was wheeled onto the elevator. *And God...please help me through this too.*

The doctors pronounced Jack's procedure a complete success. Already the pain in his chest was gone, and he was feeling relieved and deeply grateful. He was looking forward to seeing Emma and John again.

But when he got back to the room, it was empty. The bed next to his had been stripped of its sheets, and none of John's personal items remained in the room. With a growing sense of dread, Jack questioned the nurse: "What happened to the old couple?"

"The man died around noon while you were with the doctor," the nurse answered indifferently.

Tears unexpectedly flooded Jack's eyes. He could neither explain nor contain his grief. Somehow, the death of the old man who had been so dearly loved left him feeling emptier than he could have imagined. Suddenly he felt a strong need to talk to his parents.

Jack found his cell phone and called his parents, letting them know about his emergency and that everything would be OK. "Jack, you should have called. I would have added this procedure to my prayers for you," his mom said.

"I know," Jack replied. "See you in a couple of days." Before his mom could respond, Jack said good-bye, tears filling his eyes. "I'll pray for you. I love you."

He didn't know if it had been the medicine or the angioplasty, but something had definitely affected his heart. He liked the way it felt. He hoped it would last forever.

The next morning Jack waited anxiously for the doctor to sign off on his release. Suddenly he knew what he wanted to do. The deep needs of this elderly woman had awakened in him the quality that all heroes seem to possess—compassion.

Grabbing his cell phone, he speed-dialed his office and left a message for his assistant. "I'm doing OK. Everything went well, and I'm getting ready to go home. Listen. Find everything you can about a John

Vanderhassen. He just died here at the hospital. Call the funeral homes. Find out if any service is scheduled. Get a home address. Have food catered to his widow, Emma. Get me the time of the service. And give the funeral home my credit card number. Tell them to charge all the expenses to me."

I want to use this new heart God has revived within me to comfort the broken heart of a new friend, Jack thought to himself as he hung up the phone. He couldn't remember feeling this good in a very long time.

Two days later, Jack went to John's funeral and sat alone at the back of the chapel. He had postponed his urgent business trip once again and scheduled a flight for the next day to visit his parents. An elderly cleric spoke a short, well-used eulogy over John Vanderhassen as his widow, Emma,sat weeping—alone—in the front pew.

After the benediction, Emma turned and saw Jack wiping away genuine tears. Surprised, she stood up and moved down the chapel's center aisle toward him. Their eyes met,and unspoken words passed between them. Jack stood and moved toward her.

An elderly widow and a reborn businessman, no longer strangers, their lives inextricably intertwined, met halfway down the aisle and embraced. Emma started to sob, burying her face in Jack's shoulder. He held her as though she were his mother, soothing her grief and praying silently.

Emma wept for a long time, tears of gratitude mingling with tears of sorrow. Time stood still, and Jack would have stayed there all day if that were what Emma required. Jack had all the time in the world for what was truly important, and this was. He would take her to the graveside and then out for dinner.

Emma didn't know it yet, but Jack had committed himself to check on her daily by phone.He would see that she was all right and visit her when she was lonely. Maybe someday he would keep a loving vigil by her bedside as her life slipped away. He would become like a real son to her—and to his own parents. His heart was so full and happy he wondered that his chest could contain it.

勇敢的心

窗外阴暗寒冷的天气状况好像要透过半遮掩的树荫，渗透到这间半私人的医院病房里来。杰克的心情和窗外景色一样压抑、灰暗。昨天夜里，胸口的剧痛使得他不得不来到医院看急诊，现在他就躺在这家医院的心脏病监护病房里。

"心血管病，……我？……怎么可能呢……？"杰克尽力使自己接受目前的状况。尽管药物让他的疼痛减轻到不是很难受的程度，但是药物却不能缓解纠缠不休的烦恼。他的日程安排多数是满满的商务会谈，可现在一切都不受他支配了。"今天是周一……周四

早上,我得乘飞机前往芝加哥去解决位于我们中西部地区机构的合并要务。"他牙根紧咬,恼恨这个未曾安排的突发事件给他带来的严重后果。

他已经给办公室的工作人员打过电话,并且告诉秘书不要让任何人知道他急诊的事情。他不想让人探望,不需要电话问候,不要鲜花或者贺卡——更重要的是不想要别人同情。杰克想要的就是快点康复,这样的话,他就能重新回到自己的各种工作计划中去。他闭上眼睛,想把在病房里的另外两个人从他的视线中隔开。他发牢骚说:"我真不敢相信这里竟然没有可用的单人病房。"

但是,他的不安让他的眼睛不由自主地睁开了;他的目光扫视着这个房间,然后落在他的室友身上。老人年龄很大,当他通过绑在脸上的氧气面罩大口喘气的时候,几乎一动不动。他好像病得不轻,而且他的妻子又瘦又小。当她将自己骨瘦如柴的手深情地与丈夫的手相握时,看得出来她很疲惫。

这对老夫妇的行为深深震撼了他。他们对彼此的温柔和关爱是毋庸置疑的。杰克患病的心脏产生一种全新而奇特的感觉。他所有的成就、金钱和荣誉都不能让他买到这对朴实夫妇所拥有的哪怕是一丁点儿的温情。

杰克根本没有时间照顾妻子和家庭。他在大学商学院所学的知识把他带入了繁忙的职业生涯，这份事业耗尽了他的时间和情感。他很想知道，当他走到生命尽头的时候，是否会有人带着那样殷切的期望和关爱来看望他呢？是否会有人陪伴他左右，握着他的手，为他能够康复祈祷，或者为失去他而痛哭呢？如果他的心律变得越来越糟——起码来说如果他没有考虑到这种可能性，他就是个傻子——他知道自己死的时候会是一个非常可怜的人。

突然间，他再也受不了脑中的这种念头了。这让他不安，使得他的脾气更暴躁。他把这种想法抛到脑后，尽量去想商业上的事；可是杰克的目光和思想再次转向躺在旁边病床上的男人和坐在他旁边的女人。这次，他们两个人让他想起了远在2 000英里之外自己那年迈的父母。他想到这些年来他与父母待在一起的时间是何其短暂，父母又是何其孤独。这时，一股思乡之情、懊悔之意涌上心头。

杰克觉得他需要和对面的女人聊一聊。"你的丈夫怎么样了，艾玛？"

老妇人抬起头看看，吃了一惊。"我听见护士叫您艾玛。"他解释道。第一次意识到与其说他是他们中的一分子不如说他们俩是他的世界中的一部分。

杰克的回答让她感到可信，于是她回过头看了一眼她的丈夫，表情很忧伤。"不太好，"她回答道，"约翰的情况不妙，医生给他安装了心脏起搏器，但是他有不良反应，我非常担心。"她顿了顿，然后不出声了，只是默默地流泪。

正当杰克想要努力说点什么来安慰艾玛时，工作人员推着一辆手术车来了，他们要把男的推去做常规检查。"一会儿见，"他很虚弱地对艾玛说。近来杰克几乎不祈祷了，然而毫无疑问是时候恢复习惯了，应该为自己和这对孤苦伶仃的老夫妇积蓄一点精神动力。当男人被推出门外时，杰克向他们保证说："我会为你们俩祈祷的。"

当一行人走进走廊，杰克通过房间外知情的人了解到这个地位比自己低的人的名字——温德哈森。他认为这是个不同寻常的名字。……温德哈森……温德哈森……一瞬间,他觉得记住这个名字非常重要。

"上帝,请保佑艾玛和约翰·温德哈森吧,"杰克一边默默地祈祷,一边被推进了电梯,"上帝……也请您帮我度过这一关。"

医生宣布杰克的常规治疗非常成功。现在他胸口的疼痛已经没有了,他感觉很轻松并且满怀深深的感激之情。他现在就盼望着能再次见到艾玛和约翰。

然而,当他回到病房里时,病房里空无一人。他旁边的病床的床单已经换掉了,而且房间里没有留下任何一件约翰的私人物品。杰克心里升起一种不祥的预感,他问护士:"那对老夫妇怎么样了?"

"临近中午前,当你和医生在一起的时候,男的死了。"护士漠然地答道。

太不可思议了,杰克泪水满面。他无法解释更无法抑制自己的悲痛。有点莫名其妙,不知怎的这位被人挚爱着的老人的去世让杰克感到无比空虚失落,并且这感觉比他预想的要强烈得多。突然,他心里有种强烈的愿望想和自己的父母说话。

杰克找到手机给父母打电话，想让他们知道自己出现的紧急状况，并安慰他们一切都会好的。"杰克，你早就该打电话给我们了。那样的话我会把这次治疗情况加入到我的祷告当中，为你祈祷。"他的妈妈说。

"我明白的，"杰克答道。"过几天再见。"还未等他的妈妈回话，杰克说声再见就把电话挂了，眼里充满了泪水。"我会为你们祝福的。我爱你们。"

他不清楚是药物的作用还是心脏手术的原因，然而某些东西确确实实地影响了他的心灵。他喜欢这种感觉，希望这种感觉将永远延续下去。

第二天早晨，杰克焦急地等待医生给他在出院证明上签字放行。这时，他清楚自己想做些什么。这位老妇人的强烈愿望唤醒了他内心的高贵品质，这是所有英雄人物都具备的品质——仁慈之心。

他迅速抓起电话速拨办公室的号码，然后给他的秘书留下口信："我现在很好，一切正常，现在我正准备回家。听好了！找到你所能查到的关于一个叫约翰·温德哈森的人的一切资料。他刚刚在这家医院病逝。打电话给举行葬礼的人家。问问是否所有的准备工作都安排妥当了。拿到家庭住址。置办好酒席给她的遗孀，叫艾玛。把举行葬礼的时间告诉我。还有把我的信用卡号码给办葬礼的人家，告诉他们所有的花费由我来付账。"

"我要用上帝在我内心唤醒的这颗新心来安抚一个新朋友那颗忧伤的心。"杰克边挂电话边自我思量着。很长时间以来他不记得曾经感觉这么好过。

两天后，杰克去参加约翰的葬礼，独自坐在小礼堂的后面。他已经是第二次推迟他的紧急商务旅行了，而且已经安排好第二天乘飞机去看望父母。一位上了年纪的牧师对着约翰·温德哈森的棺木讲了一段简短而流利的悼词，这个时候，艾玛孤独地坐在前排长椅上落泪。

接受完祝福之后，艾玛转过身看见杰克正在抹眼泪，非常真诚。她很惊讶地站起身，沿着教堂中央的过道朝他走去。他们四目相对，传递着不言而喻的话语。杰克起身迎向她。

　　一个上了年纪的寡妇与一个获得新生的商人，他们不再是陌生人，他们的生命不可避免地联系在一起，他们在过道的中途相会，两人紧紧相拥。艾玛把头伏在杰克的肩上开始抽泣。他抱住她就像抱住自己的母亲一样，同时安慰她的悲痛，并默默地祈祷。

　　艾玛哭了好长时间，感激的泪水与悲伤的泪水融合在一起。时间也似乎停滞了，如果艾玛请求让杰克待一天，他会那么做的。杰克把这个世界上所有的时间都用来应付真正重要的事情，这件事也是一样。他要把她带到墓地旁边，然后出去吃饭。

　　艾玛还不知道这件事情，而杰克一直亲自打电话问候她的日常生活。他要知道她一切安好，并且当她孤独的时候他就去看望她。也许，有一天当她的生命渐渐消逝，他会守在她的床边，一直细心地陪伴并关爱着她。他会像她的亲儿子一样对待她——对他的父母也是一样。他的心里很满足很幸福，他为自己的心胸能够容纳下那么多东西而感到满足和欣喜。

Heroes Go Beyond

Chapter

3

3

英雄超凡脱俗

You are blessed when you persevere under trial. You're hard pressed on every side,   but not crushed; perplexed,   but not in despair;   persecuted,   but not abandoned; stuck down, but not destroyed.

当你面对磨难坚韧不拔时,你是神圣的。你全身承受着方方面面的压力,然而你没有被压垮;你困惑迷茫,然而你没有绝望;你受到压迫,然而你没有屈服;你被打倒,然而你并没有被摧毁。

Your momentary trials are obtaining a glory that will definitely be worth all of your sacrifices. And remember…all things are possible with Me on your side.

LOVE,
YOUR GOD OF ALL COMFORT
—from James 1:12; 2 Corinthians 4:8–9, 17;
Romans 8:18; Matthew 19:26

你眼前的磨难定会收获辉煌，毋庸置疑这辉煌与你所有的付出是等价的。那么，请记住……有我在你身边，一切皆有可能。

爱，
尊贵的万能安慰之神
——摘自《雅各书》1:12;2《科林多书》4:8—9,17;
《罗马书》8:18;《马太福音》19:26

Most heroes, when applauded or commended for their heroism, simply exclaim, "I was only doing my job," or, "Anyone would have done what I did."

Perhaps that's true, but it still doesn't diminish the extraordinary effort and bravery demonstrated at a time of crisis or need. Heroes go beyond the ordinary and achieve the extraordinary. They grab hold of the impossible and do it. They go beyond what can be expected of them to sacrifice, invest, give, or do.

What empowers a hero to "go beyond"? An inner faith that sees the impossible as being possible. An inner love that puts others above self. An inner hope that believes that one person can make a difference in the world.

Heroes are simply ordinary people— like you—who do extraordinary things not because they have to but because supernatural power within lifts them beyond what's expected into the realm of the extraordinary and the miraculous!

当人们对英雄的英勇行为鼓掌喝彩或者

赞不绝口时，大多数英雄人物只是淡淡地说："我只

是做了我分内的事，" 或者，"任何人都会做我所做的

事的。"

也许没错,然而,这仍旧不会抹杀英雄们在危急时

刻或者别人需要时所体现出来的超乎寻常的努力和

勇气。英雄超越寻常人,取得杰出成就。他们不

失时机,紧紧抓住似乎不可能的事,进而

变其为可能。他们往往能够付出

别人不能付出的代价去做

出牺牲、投资、施

舍或者

行动。

　　是什么力量使英雄"超乎寻常"呢?是一种内在的

信仰:将不可能当作可能;是一种内在的爱:将别人置

于自己之上;更是一个希望:坚信一个人可以在世上创造

非凡。

　　英雄其实都是凡人——就和你我一样——

他们做出杰出成就并不是被迫的，而是因

为他们潜在的神奇力量将他们带

离并超越凡人所期待的寻常

之事,并将其带入非凡

奇迹般的领

域!

Courage is ot the absence of fear, but the capacity to move forward,confidently trusting the Maker of the heavens to cover us with the shadow of His mighty hand—even if the sky should fall.

—Susan Duke

勇气不是恐惧的缺乏而是前进的动力；我们要满怀信心，信任创造天堂的上帝会用它强而有力的手掌为我们遮风挡雨——即使天塌下来也会如此。

——苏珊·杜克

当比尔看见火苗从米莉家的窗户窜出来并且将吉姆包围住时,他迅速地爬上梯子。

When Bill saw the flames leap out of Millie's window and engulf Jim, he raced up the ladder.

Ladder Rescue

★ ★ ★ ★ ★ ★ ★ ★ ★ ★ ★ ★ ★ ★ ★

Millie woke up coughing. Her first thought was, *Not the flu again.* But then she smelled it. Smoke! She forced her eyes open. The deadly black intruder blanketed her room so thickly that she couldn't even see the door. She could feel the acrid smoke filling her lungs. Rising panic and smoke made breathing—difficult for Millie even on a good day—almost impossible. Ninety-one and confined to a wheelchair, Millie knew she didn't have the strength or mobility to outdistance the rapidly encroaching smoke and fire.

Would anyone come for her before it was too late? Millie was grateful she had fallen asleep watching television in her wheelchair and not in her bed. At least she was mobile should someone come to rescue her. But Millie had already come to the conclusion that no one could help her. She was all too aware that her rickety wooden home—even older than Millie herself— was a firetrap that should have been condemned years ago. It would have been, had there not been a shortage of retirement homes and nursing care centers in her small town of Smithton.

Smithton was a tiny dot on the map that had seen more prosperous days during the mining boom of the late 1800s.That was when the old five-story Smithton Hotel had been built from trees felled at the mine site. The old wooden structure had been updated a few times over the years with a new kitchen and an elevator that was less than reliable. But the building's quaint character and furnishings had gone largely unchanged since just after the Great Depression. That was perhaps the hotel's greatest appeal to its elderly residents—everything about the home reminded them of a time many years ago when they were young, hopeful, and just starting out. Now it was the Smithton Hotel's biggest danger.

These are my final moments, Millie thought with a

strange combination of astonishment and acceptance. There was a tinge of sadness as she realized that no one was left to mourn her death. An only child who had never married, it had been years since Millie had been part of a family. *I've lived a long, good life, though,* Millie consoled herself with a touch of pride. She sank back into her wheelchair, squeezed her eyes tightly shut, then prayed. She was ready to die.

In the blackness that engulfed her consciousness, Millie was oblivious to the firehouse siren's blaring. But several streets away, two men Millie had never met heard it and swung instantly into action.

Bill and Jim had been volunteer firefighters in Smithton for more than ten years, but they'd been friends since their earliest school days. They had played ball together, double-dated, and they still attended the same Sunday school class. They worked together at the hardware store on Main Street: Bill owned the store, and Jim Was his salesman and book-keeper.

When the siren rang, both ran out of the store and down to the end of the street. Small towns have some advantages,and the close proximity of Smithton's fire station to every building in town was one of them.

"I'll bet it's the old hotel," Bill shouted as they raced to meet the rest of the crew at the fire station.

"You're right," Jim pointed up to the part of the Smithton Hotel that could be seen beyond the single-story hard-ware store. "Look at the smoke pouring from those windows! "

The crew assembled in minutes, and the hook-and-ladder truck raced to the burning building. Handfuls of elderly residents and staff stood or sat in wheelchairs across the street. It was obvious that the entire building soon would be engulfed. Already the street-level entrances were blocked by blistering flames. Jim shuddered and hoped everyone had managed to escape.

But an agitated young woman dressed in white broke from the crowd and ran toward the firefighters. "Mildred Cox is still in there," she shouted to Jim. "She's on the fifth floor. We couldn't get to her room. The fire was too hot, and the stairway is filled with flames."

"I'm going up the ladder," Jim announced resolutely to Bill.

Bill positioned the ladder right below Millie's window, and Jim scurried up the rungs. At the top, he could only see black smoke filling the room. As soon as he broke the window with his axe, the outside air gave the internal blaze new life. Flames raced across the room, engulfing Jim in a roar of blistering heat.

Even with his mask, fire suit, and oxygen, Jim couldn't move forward. The fire blazed so fiercely that his only available path seemed to be back down the ladder. *No way I'm going back,* Jim thought. The fiery heat was now penetrating his suit, and smoke was beginning to seep through his mask. His eyes burning and swelling shut from smoke, his gloves burned through and his hands scorched, Jim lunged through the broken glass and onto the floor. It was ablaze like a charcoal grill.

The heat was so intense that Jim feared he'd never get out alive. He knew he only had seconds to locate the missing woman. Blinded by smoke, he could only feel his way through the room. Jim tripped. A bed. Feeling his way around the burning bed, he bumped into Millie's wheelchair. He reached for her. She wasn't in it!

Dropping to his hands and knees, Jim groped along the floor until he finally bumped into a human form. It was Millie. She felt lifeless, but he couldn't stop to find out for sure. Lifting Millie over his shoulder, Jim crawled back toward the window. He couldn't stand up because flames from the ceiling made survival only possible a few inches off the floor—which itself was burning all around him.

By the time he neared the outside wall, Jim's mask was filled with smoke. His burned hands and knees made every movement torture. Millie's dead weight on his shoulder and back felt like a ton. Only grim determination drove him forward. Then the room swirled around him, and Jim collapsed...just inches from the window.

When Bill saw the flames leap out of Millie's window and engulf Jim, he raced up the ladder. At the top, the heat and smoke were so intense that he couldn't enter the room. "Jim! " he shouted at the top of his lungs. But there was no answer. No one could have been heard above the thunderous roar of the fire.

He couldn't go forward, but he wouldn't retreat. Bill felt helpless. He could think of nothing rational to do to save them. So he did something irrational. With all his strength,he threw himself into the flames and landed at the foot of the window. By sheer luck or God's grace, he landed right on top of Millie and Jim. Both were unconscious. Somehow,Bill managed to cradle Millie in his right arm while dragging Jim with his left. Draping Jim over the window sill, Bill carried Millie down the ladder to the waiting arms of the sheriff.

Looking back up, Bill saw something that sent a chill up his spine in spite of the overwhelming heat. The window frame over which Bill had draped Jim's limp body was now on fire around him. Bill ran back up the ladder and pulled Jim onto his shoulders. Immediately the whole window casing collapsed, leaving the ladder with the truck as its sole support as it swung free of the building. Carefully balancing himself and his precious cargo, Bill inched his way down the ladder, falling exhausted into the arms of waiting paramedics. Minutes later, from a safe distance across the street, Bill watched the entire building collapse.

Bill and Jim had gone above and beyond the call of duty on the day of the fire and definitely qualified as heroes. But their heroics didn't stop there. Millie was in the hospital for two weeks after the fire. Bill and Jim paid for all of her medical expenses. And every day, they stopped by to visit and check on her progress.

They discovered Millie had yet another problem. When she was ready to leave the hospital, she would have no place to go. With their home gone, the Smithton Hotel's other residents were staying with family or friends until a new retirement home could be built. But Millie had no family or friends.

The two men wanted to be Millie's heroes again. Jim had an extra bedroom at his house. Bill's and Jim's wives agreed to help the guys cook, clean, do laundry, and sit with Millie. Just a month after the fire, Millie moved in at Jim's and was adopted into a new, loving family.

Millie couldn't believe that anyone would do for her what Jim and Bill had done and continue to do. "I thought I was a goner," she tells everyone who will listen to her amazing story. "It looked like I had lost everything, but gained something I never expected. Those boys are more than heroes to me...they're family! "

悬梯大营救

米莉一阵咳嗽，从梦中醒来。她首先想的是："不是又感冒了吧？"然而，她用鼻子闻了闻——是烟！她强迫自己睁开眼睛，浓重的黑色烟雾遍及她的整个房间以至于她连门都看不到。她能够感觉到刺激性的烟雾正往她的肺里钻，不断上升的恐慌和烟雾使她几乎窒息（即使是在晴好的天气米莉呼吸也很困难）。她已经91岁了，又坐在轮椅上，米莉清楚地知道她没有力气来穿过滚滚而入的烟雾和大火。

会有人在事情恶化之前来救她吗？米莉庆幸自己不是睡在床上而是坐在轮椅上看着电视睡着的。至少，假如有人来救她的话她

还可以动。然而米莉很快得出结论：没有人会来救她。她太清楚她那摇摇欲坠的木屋——甚至要比她自己都老——就是一个在几年前就该废弃的易燃堆。房子是本应该废弃的，而且在她居住的史密斯顿的小镇上根本不缺退休所和疗养院。

史密斯顿镇在地图上就是一个小点，而在19世纪晚期，采矿业迅速发展的时期它就开始呈现出更加繁荣的景象。就是在那个时候，人们用在矿区上砍倒的树建造了这个老式的高5层的史密斯顿旅馆。这栋老式木制结构建筑曾在几年的时间里翻新过几次，装修了厨房还安了电梯，但电梯不太好用。然而，这些建筑古雅的特征和陈设自从大萧条之后就因为已经没有太大的变化而过时了。可能是由于这家旅馆对那些年龄稍大的住户有着极大的吸引力——跟这个家有关的一切都让他们回忆起许多年前的某个时期，当时他们年轻，充满希望，而且初出茅庐，初入社会。现在史密斯顿旅馆最大的危险也就在于此。

"这是我最后的时刻了，"米莉想，头脑中充斥着惊叹与无奈的感受。当她意识到没有任何人留下为她的去世而悲伤时，她有一点淡淡的忧伤。她是独生女，一生未结过婚，曾经是一个家庭的一分子，可那已经是好多年前的事了。"我长寿而且过得很好，不管怎样，"米莉带着一种自豪的感动之情安慰着自己。她身子下沉坐回到轮椅上，强迫自己将眼睛紧紧闭上然后祈祷。她准备迎接死神降临了。

黑暗之中，她的意识也被吞噬了，米莉没有听到消防车警笛的尖叫声。但是就在几条街之外，两个米莉从未见过的男人听到了报警声，并立刻向这边展开行动。

比尔和吉姆在史密斯顿镇当志愿消防员已经有十多年时间了，他们两个人从入学起就是好朋友。他们总是一起打球，出双入对地约会，还一同上了同一个周末学校的课程班。他们都在位于主街上的一家五金商店里工作：比尔是店主，而吉姆是他的售货员兼业务员。

当警笛声响起时两个人都冲出商店外，并沿着大道向街的尽头跑去。小镇有许多优势，史密斯顿镇的消防队距离镇里的每一所建筑都相当近就是其中之一。

"我敢打赌是那个老式旅馆着火了,"比尔边喊边和吉姆跑去与消防站的其他队员会合。

"没错,"吉姆手向上指着史密斯顿旅馆的一角说道。"快看正从那些窗户里冒出来的烟!"掠过这个单层的五金商店就可以看到旅馆一角。

全体消防队员几分钟后集合在一起,带吊钩和梯子的卡车急速驶向着火的建筑。有几个老年居民和工作人员在街对面站着,有的坐着轮椅。很明显整个建筑很快就会被火吞噬掉。况且街道的入口被熊熊的火苗阻断了。吉姆哆嗦着,同时希望所有的人都已经设法逃脱了。

这时,一位穿白衣服有点激动的女青年从人群中冲出来,跑向消防队员。"米尔德里德·考克斯还在里面,"她冲吉姆喊道,"她在第5层,我们不能到达她的房间。火苗太热了,而且楼道里全是火。"

"我爬梯子上去,"吉姆坚决地对比尔说。

比尔把梯子正好搭在米莉的窗户下面,然后吉姆急忙登上梯子。在梯子顶端,他只能看见满屋子的黑烟。当他把窗户用斧头打破时，外面的空气使室内的火焰获得新生。火焰冲出房子，将吉姆吞噬在烈焰的怒吼之中。

即使戴着面罩和氧气，穿着消防服，吉姆也不能前进一步。火势汹涌以至于他唯一可行的道路就只有顺着梯子退回去了。"我绝不回去。"吉姆心想。现在灼热正渗透进衣服里，烟也渐渐地透过面罩渗透进去。他的眼睛冒火，紧闭双眼防止烟熏；他的手套烧毁了，手烤焦了；吉姆冲过碎玻璃，脚踩在地板上；那样子就像一座闪闪发光的木炭架子。

温度太高了，这让吉姆担心自己再也不能活着出去。他知道他只有几秒钟时间来确定生死未卜的女人的方位。浓烟让他什么也看不见，他只能摸索着通过房间。吉姆被绊倒了——是床。他沿着着火的床摸索着路，撞到了米莉的轮椅。他伸出手去够她，她竟然不在上面！

吉姆把手放低双膝跪地，顺着地板小心摸索着，直到最后，他终于碰到一个人的身体——是米莉。她摸起来好像没有了气息，但是吉姆不能停下来搞清楚真实状况。吉姆把米莉扛在肩上朝着窗户的方向往回爬。他不能站起来，因为房顶的火苗离地板可能只有不到几英寸的距离可以逃生——况且地板本身也在围着他燃烧。

等到他接近外墙之时,吉姆的面罩里充满了烟。他烧焦了的手和膝盖使他做每一个动作都疼痛难忍。在他肩上和背上,米莉死沉死沉的,仿佛有一吨重。只有坚强的意志力推动着他前进。这时吉姆感到房间在他身边旋转,然后就突然倒下了……距离窗户只有几英寸远。

当比尔看到火苗蹿出米莉房间的窗户并且将吉姆包围时,他冲上梯子。在梯子顶端,热浪和浓烟太强了以至于他进不了房间。"吉姆!"他声嘶力竭地喊道。然而没有回音。在火焰的轰响怒吼声中根本没有人能听得到。

他不能往前走,但是他更不能撤回去。比尔感到无助。他想不出用任何理性的办法来挽救他们。于是他做了非理智的举动。他用尽全身的力气冲进火海,在窗户边上着地。不知是绝对的幸运还是上帝的恩赐,他正好落在米莉和吉姆的头顶上方。两个人都失去了知觉。尽管如此,比尔还是千方百计将米莉抱在右胳膊里同时用左胳膊拽着吉姆。他再将吉姆放在窗棂上,把米莉抱下梯子,放到等在下面的警长手里。

他回过头向上看,尽管热浪滚滚,但是比尔看见的一幕让他的脊背顿生寒意,他用来放吉姆柔软身体的窗棂现在在他身边也烧着了。比尔冲回去,爬上梯子,将吉姆搭在肩上。一瞬间,整个窗户的外框倒了下来,当它摇晃着脱离房子时,卡车上的梯子成了它唯一的支撑物。比尔小心翼翼地让自己和"宝贵的货物"保持平衡,一寸一寸地走下梯子,筋疲力尽地倒在正等在那里的救护人员的怀里。几分钟后,在街对面的一个安全距离内,比尔眼看着整座房子突然倒了下去。

比尔和吉姆在着火那天的所作所为早已跨越并超越了使命的召唤,并成了当之无愧的英雄。不过,他们的英雄事迹并没有到此结束。大火之后,米莉在医院住了两个星期。比尔和吉姆承担了她所有的医疗费用。他们每天都抽空去探望她并关注她的身体进展情况。

他们发现米莉还有另外一个难题:当她准备离开医院时,她竟没有一个地方可去。史密斯顿旅馆的其他所有住户都将和家人或朋友住在一起直到新的退休公寓建好。然而米莉没有家人甚至也没有朋友。

两个男士想再次充当米莉的英雄。吉姆的家里有一间闲置的卧室。比尔和吉姆的妻子都同意为老太太做饭、打扫卫生、洗洗涮涮，并且陪伴米莉。火灾后刚刚一个月，米莉搬进了吉姆家并住在那里。她被一个充满爱与温馨的新家庭接纳了。

米莉不敢相信任何一个人都会对她做出如比尔和吉姆的行为并且一直坚持下去。"我原以为我是一个落魄之人，"她告诉每个愿意聆听她传奇故事的人。"我好像早就失去了一切，然而我得到了某些我从未期望过的东西。这些孩子对于我来说永远不只是英雄……他们是我的亲人啊！"

Heroes
Listen

Chapter

4

4

英雄善于倾听

I've chosen you, giving you a new life! You are holy and dearly loved by Me. May compassion, kindness, humility, gentleness, and patience continue to be trademarks of your life.

我选择了你，给了你新生！我爱着你，神圣而真挚。愿仁慈、善良、谦逊、亲切和耐心始终都是你人生的标志。

I'm near anyone who calls on Me in truth. I hear your silent cries and rescue you. My law is perfect, reviving your soul. My statutes are trustworthy, making wisdom simple. My precepts are right, bringing joy to your heart. When you pursue righteousness and love, you'll find life, prosperity, and honor.

WITH ETERNAL LOVE,
YOUR GOD OF HOPE
—from Colossians 3:12; Psalms 145:18–19, 19:7–8;
Proverbs 21:21

我在任何一个诚实待我的人的身边。我听到你默默的哭泣声,我拯救你。我的规则是完美的,振作你的灵魂。我的法规是值得信赖的,让智慧简单容易。我的箴言是正确的,将快乐带进你的心里。当你追求公正与爱时,你就会找到属于自己的人生、成功和荣誉。

带着永恒的爱
尊贵的希望之神
——摘自:《歌罗西书》3:12;
《诗篇》145:18–19;19:7–8;《箴言》21:21

Heroes have the uncanny ability to listen have the to the heart, not just to the spoken word. Anyone can refuse to listen, no matter how urgent the cry from someone's soul. But taking time to listen requires heroic effort.

How so? Listening means not interrupting another person's sharing. Listening means trying to understand. Listening conveys worth and importance to the speaker. Listening means taking time to really hear before leaping into a barrage of words that analyze or criticize.

This skill is a part of

every hero's arsenal of weapons against apathy, ignorance, bigotry, and prejudice. Listening requires patient attentiveness.

Heroes have a unique ability to be quick to listen, slow to speak, and slow to anger. Heroes build bridges across the silent chasms that have kept others lonely and imprisoned in their private pain. By simply listening, heroes invite others to share without fear of rejection.

Wouldn't you like to encounter such a hero the next time you have something important or personal to share? Won't you aspire to be such a hero yourself?

英雄具有神秘的聆听心声的能力，而不仅仅是聆听别人说的话。无论来自其他人内心的恳求有多迫切，任何人都可以拒绝倾听。然而花时间来聆听需要英雄般的努力。

怎么会那样呢？倾听意味着不去打扰另一个人的一份享受。倾听意味着试着去理解，倾听意味着向说话人传递价值与重要性，意味着花时间去真正地听懂信息然后才去滔滔不绝地说出一连串分析或者评论的话。

这个技巧是每个英雄"武器库"中对付冷漠、无知、偏见和歧视的

一个组成部分。倾听需要持续耐心的注
意力。

英雄具有一种独特的能力，即：快聆听、慢发言、少生
气。英雄在沉默的情感间搭建起桥梁；这些情感让别人感
到孤独，并把他们囚禁在个人的痛苦牢狱之中。仅仅是
通过倾听这种方式，英雄们把他人在不用担心会遭
到拒绝的状态下邀请过来参与其中。

如果下次你有重要的或者私人的东西
需要与人分享，难道你不希望能够遇
到一个那样的英雄吗？难道
你自己就不渴望成为
那样的英雄
吗？

To listen to someone
who has no one to
listen to him is a very
beautiful thing.

—Mother Teresa

聆听没有听众的人的心声是一件很美的事。

　　　　　　　　　　　　　——圣母特里萨

专心的聆听可以搭建一座理解和接纳的桥梁，这是言语无法做到的。

Attentive listening could build a bridge of understanding and acceptance that words never could.

The Hero in 47B

★ ★ ★ ★ ★ ★ ★ ★ ★ ★ ★ ★ ★ ★ ★ ★

Valerie was looking forward to a quiet flight. Her plan for the cross-country trip was simple—sleep. Having worked late the night before, Valerie relished the thought of relaxing in seat 47B and sleeping until her plane started its descent into the Los Angeles airport.

Valerie's professional training had been in the field of family counseling. But after a few years of practice, she had decided that the stress of daily hearing other people's problems was too emotionally draining.

So Valerie had changed careers. Her training in personnel assessment and human resources had given her the skills to land a great-paying job as head of personnel in a prestigious firm. She enjoyed her nine-to-five job and the routine of administering tests she had developed and interviewing job candidates. Placing the right people in the right jobs gave Valerie great satisfaction.

A day rarely passed when she didn't feel grateful for her escape from her previous job and the world of other people's problems. She had counseled people with marital problems,rebellious teenagers, depressed and suicidal clients, and neurotics too paralyzed to make the simplest decisions.

She didn't miss it. The frantic, desperate, late-night phone calls had stopped. People expecting instant solutions to lifelong problems no longer sat in her office. No longer was it her responsibility to fix broken people. Her duty was to her company—to find healthy, capable, qualified workers.

Now it was time for a vacation. Valerie's family had flown to the West Coast a few days earlier. After a restful flight in solitude, Valerie planned to join them at Disneyland.

Much to her consternation, the flight was jammed full. Every seat was occupied, and Valerie found herself in an aisle seat, unable to stretch out beside a vacant spot as she had hoped.

At least I can nap, Valerie thought. She settled in and prepared to slip into pleasant dreams. Then she heard a quiet but distinct sniffle. Out of the corner of her eye, she noticed tears streaming down the face of the woman next to her. The woman was staring absently out the window, dabbing her eyes with a soggy tissue.

Sad about leaving her friend or husband, Valerie guessed, pushing down any inclination to speak to her. *She'll be over it in a few minutes,* she thought as she consciously willed herself to sleep.

But the sobbing didn't subside. In fact, what had started as a slow trickle of tears slowly intensified until she could feel the woman's sobbing shaking their seats.

I guess I should say something to comfort her, she thought. Bridging that initial gap with a stranger is never easy, but it's particularly hard when polite pleasantries

simply don't fit.   Her mind played over some of the
traditional opening lines for speaking to a stranger:

"How are you?"

"Nice day."

"What about this weather?"

"Are you going home ?"

"Don't you just hate coach?"

But nothing easy was appropriate in this situation.
Such platitudes simply don't work when the stranger
you're about to address is sobbing uncontrollably.

Saying nothing would require callousness far
beyond Valerie's weary reluctance. But saying the wrong
thing could make things worse. She would have to be
careful and play this by ear.

Valerie decided the best approach might simply be
a statement that reflected the woman's own feelings
without commentary or judgment. "I see you're crying,"
Valerie acknowledged quietly.   "You seem very sad."
Describing behavior and reflecting feelings was all Valerie
wanted to do. She didn't really want to get involved. Part
of her still hoped the woman would not want to talk and

thus relieve her of her responsibility.

At first the woman said nothing, but her sobbing did begin to lessen. Valerie waited patiently. She didn't want to intrude, but she also wanted to convey understanding and empathy. Perhaps her presence, her tone, and her concern had soothed the woman enough to stop her tears and give Valerie what she wanted most—peace and quiet.

When the woman first spoke, it was so soft that Valerie almost missed it. She strained to catch the words. "My husband and I just filed for bankruptcy," the woman said, twisting several tissues tightly in her fingers as she spoke. "Our business, our beautiful home—everything's gone. He's driving a moving truck to my parents' home. We have to live with them now." Her face reflected her anguish, and her words started spilling out faster as she continued. "We've been married thirty years, raised two kids, and now we've lost everything. We have to start over again and move back in with my parents. I feel so humiliated."

She buried her head in her hands as if to hide her

shame.   "And we can't even be together. I wanted to drive with my husband, but I can't. I have to get back immediately to start a new job." She paused, then let out her last embarrassing secret.   "It's in a fast-food re-staurant. I've never worked outside the home. I have no job skills. I'm a mom, not a short-order cook."

Valerie said nothing. She just let her talk, She couldn't really change anything or help her, and any advice she could give would be meaningless. Cheerful hopefulness would seem shallow to a woman in such a dark place. But attentive listening could build a bridge of understanding and acceptance that words never could.

"I'm June," she said. She seemed suddenly embarrassed at what she had just told to a stranger, yet unquestionably. relieved to have done so. "I don't know why I'm telling you all this," she told Valerie apolo-getically. "I guess it's easier to talk to a stranger than a friend—if I had one. It seems our friends have all deserted us. The only calls we've gotten in the last few months are from creditors and attorneys—all wanting something from us."

For the first time she really looked at Valerie and considered her as an individual, not merely a kind, listening ear. "I'm sorry," she said, realization dawning as she saw the pillow. "You must want to sleep."

"Don't worry about me," Valerie reassured her. "What's next for you?"

For more than two hours she listened to June's story. Occasionally, June would take a deep breath and sigh. Valerie would nod, murmur a quiet "Yes," and then listen as June continued her saga with new courage.

Valerie didn't sleep a wink on that late-night, cross-country flight. Her plans had changed. Her own needs had gone unmet, but she felt strangely refreshed and gratified that she had helped meet someone else's. She knew that listening to June was the most important thing she could have done. She was the right person at the right time and in the right seat—47B.

As the plane landed safely on the runway and taxied to the gate, June seemed relieved and even upbeat. "Your listening has meant so much to me," June sounded truly grateful. "I've had no one to talk to about anything important for such a long time. My husband and I are so weary of talking about what has happened and feel so powerless to change it that we often just sit for hours, staring at each other, feeling numb." She looked hopefully into Valerie's eyes. "So, what do you think?"

"I think you and your husband will make it," Valerie announced, suddenly quite confident of that. "It's a new beginning," she encouraged June. "Your past doesn't determine your future. Starting over can be a great thing."

With wide-eyed surprise, June looked at her traveling companion turned confidante. "I feel so much better," she said with a deep sigh of relief. "Thank you for listening. You'll never know how much this has meant to me. Without your intervention this would have been my last flight," she said solemnly, her eyes intense.

For the first time, Valerie's face registered that she didn't have a clue what June was talking about. So discreetly—ceremoniously—June reached into her purse and placed something into Valerie's hands. June closed her hand over Valerie's and gave it a brief but meaningful squeeze that wordlessly communicated her thanks and farewell.   Valerie watched June sling her carry-on over her shoulder and walk down the aisle to the exit. She couldn't help but notice the change in June. She walked like a new woman with a new-found strength and courage.

Valerie watched her until she was gone,   then opened her hand to examine what June had left with her. It was a small bottle of pills. She studied it curiously. The bottle contained sedatives—more than enough for a fatal overdose.

Sometimes a hero doesn't have to do much or risk a lot. Listening. Encouraging. Being there. Being willing. Such basic kindnesses don't seem like the daring acts of a hero. But at the right time, those qualities can change a stranger into a friend and enable an everyday hero to save a life.

47排B座的"聆听"英雄

瓦莱丽期待着一次安静的飞行,她对这次跨越全国的旅程的计划很简单——睡觉。由于前一天晚上工作到很晚,所以瓦莱丽坐在47排B座的座位上享受着放松的思绪;希望享受睡眠直到她这班飞机开始在洛杉矶机场降落为止。

瓦莱丽的职业培训一直是家庭顾问领域。但是经过几年实际工作之后,她已经断定,每天听别人的困惑,这种压抑感就会让人心力交瘁。

因此瓦莱丽转行了。她在人事评估和人力资源方面的训练让她有能力得到一份收入不菲的工作——在一家著名公司做人事主管。她喜欢这份朝九晚五的工作；喜欢她开发的管理测评程序；喜欢面试求职者。将适合的人放在合适的工作岗位上带给瓦莱丽极大的满足感。

换了工作后的每一天，她都未因自己从以前的工作和别人的困惑世界中解脱出来而感到欣喜不已。她曾给婚姻有问题的人以建议；曾给叛逆的青少年以忠告；曾给绝望和自暴自弃的顾客以鼓励；还曾给连最简单的决定也做不了的神经过敏患者以慰藉。

她不怀念那些。深夜里那疯狂的、歇斯底里的电话没有了。那些期望能找到迅速解决一生困惑的方法的人再也不会坐在她的办公室里了。修复那些有问题的人的心灵再也不是她的责任了。她只对她的公司负责——找到健康、能干、合格的工作人员。

现在是休假时间，瓦莱丽的家人早她几天就飞往西海岸了。独自一人平静的飞行之后，瓦莱丽打算到迪斯尼乐园找他们。

让她惊讶的是飞机坐得满满的，所有的座位都有人。瓦莱丽发现她的座位靠近过道,这样就不能按照她当初期望的那样,把身体舒展到旁边的空座上。

"至少我可以打个盹。"瓦莱丽想。她坐好,准备快速进入美梦之中,突然,她听到一阵很轻但很清楚的抽泣声。透过眼角的余光她注意到眼泪正从坐在她旁边的女人的脸上淌下来。女人正用心不在焉的眼神看着窗外,用一块湿透的纸巾抹着眼睛。

"是因远离她的朋友或者丈夫伤心吧,"瓦莱丽猜想,尽力将想与她认识的冲动压下去。"几分钟后她就会停止哭泣的。"她一边想着一边有意识地想让自己入睡。

然而,呜咽声没有平息。事实上,眼泪从一开始慢慢往下淌到变得逐渐强烈起来,后来她竟然能感觉到女人的呜咽将她们的座位都震动得颤起来。

"我想我应该说点什么来安慰她一下。"她想。跨越与一个陌生人的障碍往往很难,而当简单而有礼貌的玩笑不合时宜时,事情就会特别的难办。她头脑里闪动着几种与陌生人交谈的传统开场白:

"你好吗？"

"今天很好。"

"今天的天气怎么样啊？"

"你要回家吗？"

"你不会只是讨厌机舱吧？"

但是在目前这种情形下，什么简单的措词都不合适。当你打算与之谈话的陌生人正在难以控制地哭个不停时，那些平平常常的话根本就不管用。

什么都不说需要硬心肠，这远远超过瓦莱丽因疲倦而产生的不情愿。但是如果说错话，事情可能会更糟。她得小心翼翼地并且得保持观望。

瓦莱丽认为可以做的最好办法只是一句能够反映女人自己感受而不带评论或评判的话。"我看到你哭了。"瓦莱丽小声地说道。"你好像非常伤心。"描述行为，反映情感，就是瓦莱丽想要做的所有事情。她不想真正地介入其中。思想中部分地仍然希望女人不愿说话，那样的话她就摆脱她的责任了。

起先女人没说话，不过她的呜咽声确实开始变小了。瓦莱丽耐心地等着。她不想强人所难,但是她还想向她表达对她的理解和同情。也许是瓦莱丽的存在,也许是她的语调,或是她的关心都足以让女人得到慰藉,进而她停止流泪,给瓦莱丽最想要的东西——平和与安静。

女人一开始说话的时候声音太轻了以至于瓦莱丽几乎没听到。她尽力去听清这句话。"我和我丈夫刚刚申请了破产,"女人说,当她讲话的时候,手里紧紧地搓揉着几张纸巾。"我们的事业,我们漂亮的家—— 一切的一切都没有了。他现在正开着一辆搬家的卡车去我父母家。现在我们不得不和他们住在一起。"她的面部表情反映出她的苦闷。当她接着往下讲的时候语速开始快了起来。"我们结婚已经有30年了,养了两个孩子,而现在我们已经失去了一切。我们不得不从头再来,搬回去和我的父母一起住。我觉得太丢人了。"

她用手捂着脸好像要将羞耻隐藏起来似的。"而且,甚至我们不能在一起。我想和丈夫开车但是我不能。我必须马上赶回去开始一份新的工作。"她顿了顿,然后讲出了最后那个令人尴尬的秘密。"在一家快餐店。我从未离开家出门过。我没有工作技能。我是位母亲,不是临时厨师。"

瓦莱丽一言未发。她就是让她讲出来。她不能确实地改变任何事或者帮助她,就连她能给她的任何建议都是没有意义的。对于身处那么黑暗处境的女人来说,充满快乐的希望会显得不切实际。但是专心地倾听可以搭建一座理解与接纳的桥梁,这些是言语无法做到的。

"我叫朱尼,"她说。她好像突然间为对一个陌生人所讲的话觉得难为情,不过,毋庸置疑她因为那样做了而感到轻松。"我不知道我为什么会告诉你这些,"她对瓦莱丽深表歉意,"我想和陌生人讲话要比讲给朋友听容易得多——如果我有朋友的话。似乎我们的朋友都远离我们。在过去的几个月里,我们接到的电话都是债主和律师——全都想从我们手里要点什么。"

她头一次真真切切地看了看瓦莱丽,把她当做一个人,而不单单是一只善良的聆听耳朵。"对不起,"她说,当她看到枕头时她才回过神来。"你想必是要睡觉吧。"

"别担心我,"瓦莱丽安慰她说,"你接下来打算怎么办呢?"

两个多小时里她都在倾听朱尼的故事。偶尔,朱尼会深吸一口气然后叹息。瓦莱丽就点头,轻轻地说声"是",然后就接着听朱尼鼓足勇气继续她的传奇讲述。

在那个深夜,在那个跨越国度的飞机上,瓦莱丽一点也没有睡。她的计划改变了。她自己的需求没有得到满足,但是她觉得精神出奇的好并且很满足,因为她帮助别人满足了要求。她清楚,倾听朱尼讲话是她所做过的事中最重要的。她就是在合适的时间,在合适的座位——47排B座,出现的那个合适的人。

飞机安全着陆在跑道上开始向登机门口滑行时,朱尼似乎轻松了甚至乐观起来。"你的倾听对我来说意义太大了,"朱尼说的话听起来带着真诚的感激,"我已经好久没有跟一个人聊一些重要的事情了。我和我丈夫对谈论所发生的事情非常厌烦,并且觉得无力改变事实，以至于我们经常是几个小时地坐着，互相看着，感觉麻木了。"她满怀希望地注视着瓦莱丽的双眼。"那么你觉得怎么样？"

"我想你和你丈夫会成功的，"瓦莱丽大声说道，突然感到非常肯定。"这是新的开端，"她鼓励着朱尼，"你的过去不能决定你的将来。从头再来可能会是件好事。"

惊得目瞪口呆，朱尼眼看着她的旅伴变成知己。"我感觉好多了，"她长长地舒了口气说道，"谢谢你的倾听。你不知道这对于我来说意义有多大。如果没有你的介入，恐怕这将会是我最后的旅行了。"她严肃地说，眼神深邃。

第一次，瓦莱丽的脸上显示出她并不知道朱尼在说什么。那么小心翼翼地——是隆重地——朱尼把手伸进钱包然后把什么东西放进瓦莱丽的手心里。朱尼握住瓦莱丽的手，给了她一个简短但意义深刻的拥抱，无言地传递着对她的谢意和祝福。瓦莱丽注视着朱尼将随身背包背在肩上,穿过过道走向出口。她不能帮忙但是却注意到在朱尼身上发生的变化。她走路的样子就像一个新的具备了崭新力量和勇气的女人。

瓦莱丽目送着她直至她消失在视线里,然后张开手看看朱尼给她留下了什么东西。是一小瓶药片。她好奇地研究这瓶药。瓶里装着镇静药——超过致命的剂量。

有的时候不必做太多事或者冒太大的险。倾听。鼓励。待在那儿。心甘情愿。这些基本的仁慈行为似乎不太像英雄的英勇行为。然而在恰当的时间,那些优秀品质可以把陌生人变成朋友,并且能让一个平常的英雄挽救生命。

Heroes Carry the Burden

Chapter

5

⑤

英雄勇挑重担

I've given you every grace and blessing you need for doing My will. Don't forget that your all-surpassing power is from Me and not from you.

为了实践我的意愿，我已经给予了你需要的所有优点和祝福。别忘了你超越一切的能力来自于我而不是来自于你。

I've saved you through My gift of grace. And My grace is all that you need. My power is perfected in your weakness. I'll make all grace abound to you so that you'll always overflow in every good work.

TESTIFY TO MY AMAZING GRACE,
JESUS
—from 1 Corinthians 1:7–9; 2 Corinthians 4:7;
Ephesians 2:8; 2 Corinthians 12:9, 9:8; Acts 20:24

通过恩赐给你的优点,我拯救了你。我的恩赐全是你需要的。我的力量在你的弱点中趋于强大。我将给你大量的优点恩惠,这样你就会在做好每项工作之外表现更加出色。

证明我的惊人的恩赐
耶稣
——摘自:《科林多书》1:7-9;《科林多书》Ⅱ 4:7;
《以弗所书》2:8;《科林多书》Ⅱ 12:9,9:8;《使徒行传》20:24

In life's endless struggles, victims complain and resent the burdens they must carry. Heroes, on the other hand, find the strength not only to carry their own burdens but also to pick up the load that is crushing someone else and carry it cheerfully.

What enables a hero to carry another's burden even when that load may seem impossibly overwhelming? Heroes discover that when they give of themselves to lift someone's burden, their own weariness melts away and their strength is multiplied to accomplish the extraordinary.

Burden-bearing is more than a rational, planned response to an obvious need. It's a miraculous equation God has established by which someone else's burden, no matter how heavy, is made light for another who will come alongside and lift it from his or her bowed-down shoulders.

Be a hero today. Help to carry a burden that is weighing someone down. You'll find it's not too heavy—and that your own burdens will feel lighter as well.

在生命无休止的争斗中，深处其中的人对待他们必须承担的责任满腹牢骚并恨之入骨。另一方面，英雄们寻找力量不仅承担自己的责任而且挑起压在他人身上的重担，并且欣然承担。

是什么促使英雄即使当那个重担可能看起来重得不可思议的时候，还要继续承担另一个人的责任呢？英雄们发现，当他们全身心地扛起别人的重担时，自己的疲倦厌烦感消失得无影无踪，而且力量倍增并能够完成伟大的事业。

力量的产生与其说是一种理性不如

说是对一个显而易见的需求的有计划的反应。它是一

个神奇的方程式，上帝按照这个方程式创造了一个人的

责任,无论这个责任有多重,对于另一个将会走到其身旁

从他或者她的累弯了的肩膀上挑起这个重担的人,都

是轻的。

做个英雄,就现在。帮忙挑起把某个人压

弯了腰的重担吧。你会发现这重担并

不太重——你还会感觉到,

自己的担子也轻了

很多。

Manage them and our hands
become instruments of
grace—not just tools
in the hands of God, but
God's very hands.

—Max Lucado

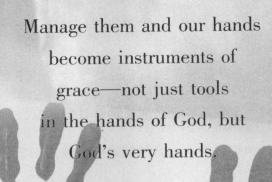

管理他们，那么我们就会变成恩赐的工具——不仅仅是上帝手里的工具，而本身就是上帝的手。

——马克斯·卢卡多

在成功的外科手术后，李的外科医生告诉克里斯："我不清楚你是怎么做到的，但是你救了你哥哥的命。"

Lee's *surgeon addressed Chris after the successful surgery.* "*I don't know how you did it, but you saved your brother's life.*"

Strength of a Brother's Love

★ ★

The long, sultry, holiday weekend in July was marked by warm afternoon showers. But nothing seemed to dampen the spirits of the large crowd of music lovers at the festival on the Illinois State Fairgrounds. Country, bluegrass, southern gospel, and contemporary Christian music had delighted the enthusiastic crowd. Lee and his fellow band members had thoroughly enjoyed their gig. The added bonus was renewing old friendships with other bands, many of whom they only saw once a year at this festival.

Music was Lee's hobby. Now Sunday was fast disappearing, and Monday's approach brought thoughts of real-world responsibilities. Like every band member, Lee had a family and a job waiting back home in Georgia. He was due at work early Monday morning. His younger brother, Chris, had an early morning class. Visiting, eating, swapping stories, and playing music late into the previous two nights had been fun, but now everyone was tired and eager to get home. Happy but exhausted, the band loaded their trailer and prepared the fifteen-passenger rental van for the long drive home.

John, the group's manager, drew the first shift behind the wheel. He had gotten the most sleep the night before—four hours. Phil, the band's sound technician, rode shotgun.He would drive the second shift when John got tired. Five band members competed to be able to "stretch out" and sleep on one of the four bench seats on the eleven-hour ride home. The flip of a penny determined which unlucky musician would have to settle for a twin-sized foam mattress pad laid on the floor between two of the seats. After one last big dinner of fried chicken, they left the fairgrounds, settled into their assigned places, and headed toward home.

At first, the emotional euphoria of their exciting weekend kept everyone awake, pumped up, and reliving memories.Even so,   John decided it wouldn't hurt to pull through a nearby restaurant's drive-through for a large cup of coffee. As they waited in line to pick up the drink, the lack of sleep caught up with them.   A profound but pleasant weariness settled on the passengers.   By the time John pulled away from the drive-in window, everyone else was fast asleep.

John sipped his coffee,   put on a favorite CD,   and cranked up the sound and the air conditioning,   hoping the combination of caffeine,   noise,   and cool air would make it easier to stay alert.   He drove south on the interstate,   determined to enjoy the drive as he sang along with familiar songs.

The first hour was uneventful. Traffic was unexpecte-dly light for a holiday weekend,   and the scenery was pleasant but somewhat monotonous and mesmerizing. Tired of the CD, John searched the radio for some decent music or a controversial talk show.   Finding neither,   he turned off the radio and settled back into his own private musings.

Lost in thought,   John tuned out the boredom of driving.   He found himself on autopilot driving through some road construction.   His alertness waned,   and his drowsiness grew. *I need to pull over and let Phil drive for a while,* he thought.

He turned to ask Phil to relieve him, but his co-pilot was sleeping soundly, head buried in a pillow pressed against the window. When John looked back at the road, he realized the van had drifted toward the right edge. He quickly pulled the steering wheel to the left to correct his course.

But the construction had left the road's shoulder significantly lower than the driving lanes. The van's right front tire caught the edge of the pavement and, after a brief moment of resistance, overshot the road to the left shoulder. The van skidded left through the loose gravel strewn on the shoulder. John's adrenaline kicked in, and he jerked the van's steering wheel sharply to the right in a desperate and instinctive attempt to keep the unwieldy vehicle on the road. But the tire abruptly caught the pavement's edge at a speed of more than sixty miles per hour. By now the back trailer had begun to jackknife, making it impossible to control the van or even predict its movement.

Horrified, John was the only one awake to recognize their impending danger before the van and trailer rolled over in the wide, grassy median. The sleepers were jolted awake. Their unrestrained bodies flew through the air, impacting first one surface, then another. The grinding of metal and shattering of glass were deafening. Friction caused the smell of hot metal, and the air was thick with pulverized particles as the rolling van skidded upside down, windows popping out along the way.

And then it was over. The van teetered, then was motionless. For a moment the air was eerily silent, then there were moans of pain. Chris quickly evaluated his own condition, already aware of a multitude of bumps, bruises, and cuts. His right arm ached when he tried to move it, but he didn't appear to be seriously hurt. Immediately he thought of the others.

"Is everybody OK?" Chris shouted. Quickly he called out each band member's name. Three of the guys had neck injuries and hurt too much to move.

"I'm stuck here," Phil moaned. The van had come to rest on its passenger side. Phil's door was pinned shut by the ground, and his seat belt and the awkward position of his seat trapped him. John had been knocked unconscious and had a deep, bleeding gash on his forehead.

Everyone was accounted for except Chris's brother Lee. Chris shoved aside his own pain and rising panic. He knew he must find Lee and help him. With great effort, Chris pulled himself out of a bent and glassless window directly above his head on the driver's side. Sitting atop the overturned van, he felt a sharp pain in his right ankle. *I must have been slammed against the seat in front of me and really hurt my right arm and ankle,* Chris thought as he tried to clear the shock from his brain and focus on what he had to do.

"Lee! Lee, are you all right?" Chris shouted. No one answered. Ignoring the pain in his arm and ankle, Chris lowered himself to the grass. Dragging himself around the van, he searched for Lee.

Then he heard a weak moan from the ground near the back of the van. Chris moved toward the sound with both hope and dread. Hope was replaced by horror when he spotted his brother's arm under the van's right rear wheel. Lee had been thrown from the van and pinned beneath it.

Forgetting his own condition and the laws of physics, Chris stood and pushed against the massive van. It didn't budge.

"I can hardly breathe," Lee whispered with labored difficulty.

"Hold on," Chris pleaded.

Lee was a slender, six-foot, 160-pound rail of a guy who didn't have any fat to cushion him from the crushing weight of the van. Desperate, and with a strength far beyond himself, Chris used his good left arm to lift the wheel. In an instant, he grabbed Lee's extended arm with his own injured right arm. Screaming in pain, Chris lifted and pulled with more than everything in him. He felt consciousness slip away as he descended into total blackness.

The first rescue worker on the scene was a county sheriff. What he saw sickened him. He found five young men in the van and two lying on the grass about a yard away. All appeared seriously injured and by that time were unconscious.

When paramedics arrived, they rushed first to the broken and fragile-looking man lying near the van's rear tire. They revived Lee. "I...can't...breathe," Lee gasped, barely conscious. Recognizing the seriousness of Lee's condition, paramedics evacuated him and Chris by helicopter to the nearest major hospital.

During the fifteen-minute ride, Lee clung to life, barely breathing. Chris had come to and now directed his remaining strength toward encouraging his brother: "Lee, hang in there. I'm praying, bro. Don't give up."

At the hospital, Chris refused medical treatment for himself until he was sure he had done all he could for his brother. He learned that a broken rib had pierced Lee's left lung. The weight of the van had crushed his hip. He was bleeding internally. His spleen had ruptured. Lee was in serious condition, and Chris insisted on staying with him until doctors rushed his brother into surgery.

It was a miracle no one had been killed. The three men with injured necks would recover slowly over the next two months. John had a mild concussion and required stitches in his forehead. None had any serious or lasting injuries.

But when the details of what had happened were pieced together, there was little doubt there had been a second miracle. X-rays revealed that Chris had broken his ankle and right arm. Heroically, he had found the courage and strength to block out his pain, lift a fifteen-passenger van with one arm, and pull Lee out from under it with the other.   Six paramedics,   two police officers,   and a sheriff had worked the accident scene. Trying to free Phil,   who was trapped inside,   these nine men had tried to accomplish what Chris had somehow managed by himself.   But they couldn't.   It took a tow truck to lift the van off its side and free Phil.

"Son,"   Lee's surgeon addressed Chris after the successful surgery.   He shook his head in amazement at the young man on crutches with casts on his arm and leg.   "I don't know how you did it,   but you saved your brother's life.   If he had been left under that van until the rescuers arrived,   he surely would have suffocated to death."

That day,   an ordinary man reached down inside and found something extraordinary to help his brother in need. More than his brother's keeper, Chris became his brother's hero!

兄弟手足情

午后一场温暖的阵雨见证着七月这个漫长、闷热而欢乐的周末。但是,好像没有什么能降低在伊利诺斯州露天游乐场上参加节日庆祝活动的这一大群音乐发烧友们的激情。乡村美景、牧草、南部信仰以及当代基督教的音乐都令这群活力四射、充满激情的人兴奋万分。李和同队的乐队成员完全沉浸在他们的欢乐中。另外的好处就是能和其他乐队重叙老友之情,有许多乐队的人一年只有在这次节日庆典上才能见一面。

音乐是李的业余爱好。现在周日正在很快过去,而即将到来的周一让他想起现实世界中的责任。同每个乐队成员一样,李在乔治亚州有个家庭和一份工作正等着他。他得在周——大早就工作。他的弟弟克里斯清早要上课。访客,吃东西,互相讲故事,以及前两天晚上演奏音乐到很晚,这些都很有意思,但是现在每个人都累了,都盼着回家。高兴但是筋疲力尽。一队人装满他们的拖车,准备好租来的可以容纳15人的篷车,准备远行回家。

约翰,乐队的经纪人,坐在驾驶位上开第一班车。他前一天晚上睡的觉最多——4个小时。菲尔,乐队的音响师,端着猎枪。当约翰开累了,他开第二班。5名乐队成员争着舒展自己的身体分别躺在4个长形座位中的其中一个上,即将度过11个小时的回家之旅。他们扔硬币来决定是哪个倒霉的乐师不得不将一个双人大小的泡沫床垫铺在两个座位中间的地上,躺在上面。吃了最后一顿炸鸡大餐之后,他们离开露天游乐场,躲进已分配好的位置,朝着家的方向出发了。

起先,令人兴奋的周末带来的自我陶醉感让他们都睡不着,他们说个不停并回味着记忆中的往事。即使那样,约翰觉得把车开进附近一家餐馆的快餐部要一大杯咖啡也不会影响情绪的。当他们排队等着取饮料时,困意随即而至。一种很深但却舒服的疲倦感降临在这些旅客身上。等到约翰把车从"免下车"餐馆的橱窗旁开走时,所有的人都睡着了。

约翰一口一口地喝着咖啡,放上一张喜欢的唱片,将声音档调得很高,并将空调调得很冷,希望咖啡因、噪音和冷空气混合在一起可以让他更容易保持清醒。他顺着州际公路往南开,决定一边跟着熟悉的乐曲唱歌一边享受开车的乐趣。

头一个小时平安无事。对于一个快乐的周末来说,交通状况出奇的通畅,而且景色宜人;但是多少有点单调和让人犯困。听烦了唱片,约翰调着收音机想找一些正经音乐或者一个谈话激烈的脱口秀节目。两种节目都未找到,他关掉收音机,回到他的独自冥想中。

沉浸在思绪之中,约翰将开车的乏味驱走了。他发现自己正使用自动驾驶,车正驶过一些路旁建筑。他的警惕性减退,瞌睡感增强。"我得靠边停车然后让菲尔开一会,"他想。

他转过身去叫菲尔来换班,但是他的副驾驶正呼呼大睡,脑袋埋进一个挤靠着窗户的枕头里。当约翰回头看路时,他意识到货车已拐向路的右侧。他迅速地向左拉动方向盘想打正车道。

但是道路设施使得路肩明显低于行车道。车的右前轮胎碰撞上了人行道的边缘,瞬间的阻力之后,车子飞过路面冲向左路肩。货车向左侧滑过路肩上的沙砾。约翰的肾上腺激素急剧上升,他用力向右猛推货车的方向盘,不顾一切但是目的明确,他要把这辆不受控制的汽车保持在行驶轨道上。然而车轮突然以每小时超过60英里的速度撞向人行道旁。到这个时候,后面的拖车开始回转折合,不听使唤,这使得想要控制货车甚至判断它的运行轨迹都不可能了。

约翰惊恐万分,在货车和拖车在宽阔、杂草丛生的路中间来回翻滚以前,他是意识到他们迫在眉睫的危险的唯一清醒的人。睡觉的人被颠醒。他们不受控制的身体在空中飞舞,一个一个地叠压在一起。刺耳的金属摩擦声和玻璃破碎的声音震耳欲聋。摩擦使热金属发出刺鼻的气味,当飞驰的货车打滑翻车的时候,空气中布满碎裂的粉尘;车窗迸裂出来掉在路上。

然而,一切归于平静,货车左右摇晃着,后来就一动不动了。有一会儿,空气死一般的沉静,接着痛苦的呻吟声传出。克里斯立刻检查自己的情况,看见身上有许多碰伤,瘀伤和划伤。当他试着动弹时右臂有疼痛感,不过他好像受伤不太重。他立即想起其他的队友。

"大家都好吗?"克里斯叫着,很快,他叫出了每一个队友的名字。有3个人脖子受伤太重动不了。

"我被卡在这了,"菲尔呻吟着说。货车已经侧翻过来了。菲尔那边的车门被地面别住了,他的安全带和不太方便的座位位置把他困住了。约翰被撞得头脑发晕,他的前额有一道很深正流血的伤口。

除了克里斯的哥哥李之外，所有人都在。约翰不顾自己的伤痛，心里升起一丝恐惧。他知道，他一定要找到李并帮助他。费了很大的劲，克里斯从位于头顶上，已经变形，没了玻璃的车的侧面窗户将自己拖出来。他坐在翻了的车顶上，感到右脚踝钻心的疼痛。"我一定是刚才猛地撞到前面的座位上了，并且确确实实地弄伤了右臂和右脚踝。"克里斯边想边尽力把恐惧从脑中驱走，把注意力集中在他要做的事情上面。

"李！李，你没事吧？"克里斯喊道。没有人回应。克里斯不顾手臂和脚踝的疼痛，俯下身趴在草地上，拖着身体围着货车转，寻找李。

突然，他听到一阵微弱的呻吟声从车后附近的地面上传来。克里斯满怀希望与恐惧朝着发出声音的方向移动。当他看到他哥哥的手臂在货车的右后轮底下的时候，希望被恐惧湮没。李被甩出车外并且被别在车轮下面了。

克里斯忘记了自身的情况和物理学的规律，他站起身用力推这个笨重的货车。货车纹丝不动。

"我快不能呼吸了，"李小声地说，感到有千斤重担压在身上。

"坚持住，"克里斯恳求道。

李是个身体瘦长，身高6英尺，体重160磅，电线杆一样的小伙子。他身上没有任何多余的脂肪来做缓冲，保护自己免受货车的重压。克里斯不顾一切地使出远超出自身的力量，用他完好的左臂抬起车轮。瞬间，他用自己受伤的右手抓住李伸出来的手臂。疼痛中一声尖叫，克里斯抬起远远超过他自身的重量。当他倒下眼前一片漆黑的时候，他感到意识也迅速消失了。

在出事地点的第一个救援者是一个乡村的警长。他看到的景象让他差点昏过去。他发现货车里有5个男青年，有2个躺在离车一码远的草地上。所有人看起来都伤得很重，并且当时都不省人事。

救护人员到来时，他们先冲向躺在货车后轮旁边的受伤严重、脸色难看的人。他们把李弄醒。"我……不能……呼吸，"李意识模糊，喘息着说。意识到李的状况的严重性，医护人员用直升机把他和克里斯送到最近的较大医院。

在15分钟的飞行期间,李生命垂危、奄奄一息。克里斯苏醒过来,现在他把仅存的力气都用在鼓励他的哥哥上:"李,坚持住,我在祈祷,哥哥。千万别放弃。"

在医院,克里斯直到确定自己已经为他的哥哥做了一切他能做的事才接受为自己进行药物治疗。他了解到,一根断了的肋骨插进了李的左肺,货车的重压把他的坐骨压碎了,他内出血,脾也破裂了。李的情况很严重,克里斯坚持要陪伴他,直到医生把他的哥哥推进外科手术室。

没有人员死亡是个奇迹。脖子受伤的3个人会在接下来的两个多月里慢慢康复的。约翰有轻度的脑震荡并且需要在前额上缝几针。没有人有任何严重或者永久性的损伤。

然而,当事故发生的细节被一点点拼凑在一起时,人们有个小小的疑问:当时有一秒钟的奇迹发生。透视显示克里斯脚踝和右手臂骨折。如英雄传奇般,他鼓足勇气,凝聚力量将疼痛置之度外,只手抬起了一个可容15名乘客的货车,并将李从车底下拉出来,其他几个人还在车里。6名医护人员,2名警官连同一位警长处理了事故现场。为了使深陷车内的菲尔脱困,这9个人曾竭尽全力想做到克里斯自己一个人不知靠什么力量做到的抬车这件事。但是他们没有成功。他们用拖车才把货车拖离侧面,这才彻底解放了菲尔。

"好小子,"李的外科医生在手术成功后对克里斯说道。他惊讶地冲着这个手和脚都缠着绷带拄着拐杖的年轻人直摇头。"我不清楚你是怎么做到的,但是你救了你哥哥的命。如果他一直待在那辆货车底下直到救援人员到来,那么他肯定早就闷死了。"

那一天,一个普通人走入内心深处,寻找到非同寻常之物来挽救他那需要帮助的哥哥。与其说克里斯是他哥哥的守护者,不如更确切地说他是他哥哥的英雄。

Heroes
Are
Courageous

Chapter
6

6

英雄虎胆龙威

Never fear people

or circumstances, for I am
with you! I'll strengthen
you and help you.

千万别害怕人
或者事，
因为有我伴你左右！我
会让你力量倍增并向
你伸出援手。

I'll uphold you with My righteous right hand.
Don't be overcome by evil. Instead, take a
stand, overcoming evil with good. I'm your
guide, even to the end.

YOUR GOD

—from Isaiah 41:10; Romans 12:21; Psalm 48:14

我会用我充满正义的右手扶助你。千万不要
被邪恶征服。相反,坚持立场,用善良征服邪
恶。我为你指引道路直到最后。

你的上帝

——摘自《以赛亚书》41:10;《罗马书》12:21;

《诗篇》48:14

Life is filled with tests. Those tests are opportunities for powerful testimonies to God's faithfulness to grant us the strength and courage necessary to overcome every obstacle and to finish strong. A hero's courage is demonstrated in the midst of danger and crisis. Heroes refuse to avoid life's confrontations with evil. Rather, heroic courage faces the test, resolutely attacks every obstacle, and perseveres to the best of its ability.

Perhaps the greatest battle each hero must fight is against discouragement. An impending crisis or trial threatens defeat. Cowards cower before the enemy and retreat. The weak crumble under attack. Discouragement causes its victims to falter, believing all is lost.

But heroes know that, nothing is impossible in the world. They believe they can overcome in spite of overwhelming odds. Armed with the indomitable weapon of courage, heroes march into battle convinced that the battle is worth any cost or sacrifice. Such men and women stand firm and serve as examples who inspire others to carry on with courage.

人生充满磨难。那些磨难就是机遇，就是

强大的圣经出于对上帝的忠诚赐予我们力量和必需的

勇气，我们要战胜一切艰难险阻，让自己成长壮大。一位

英雄的勇气是在危险和危机之中得到证实的。英雄的生

命中拒绝逃避与邪恶对抗。相反，英雄鼓起勇气直面磨

难，坚决地对抗一切艰难困苦并坚持不懈，直到能力

提高到最强状态。

也许每个英雄必须参加的最大战斗

是对抗沮丧，一场迫在眉睫的危

机或者暂时性的威胁、挫

折。懦夫在敌人

面前退

缩逃跑。意志薄弱之人在受到攻击时粉身碎骨。沮丧会使受其影响者胆怯,同时觉得失去了一切。

然而,英雄们知道世上没有做不到的事,一切皆有可能。他们坚信即使是无法抵抗的难事怪事,他们也能够征服。英雄们装备上勇气这个不屈不挠的有力武器迈步向前进入战场,并且坚信这场战斗值得为其付出任何代价甚至牺牲。无数这样的男人和女人坚毅挺立着为他人服务,这些鲜活的例子将激励其他人鼓起勇气继续向前。

Courage is the strength to
face pain, act under pressure,
and maintain one's values in
the face of opposition.

—Eleanor Roosevelt

勇气给人力量直面苦痛；在压力面前有所作为；在面临敌对时保持自己的尊严和价值。

——埃莉诺·罗斯福

这位士官好像没有
注意到现场的危险，
眼里只有受伤者的
迫切需要。

The *sergeant didn't*
seem to notice the
danger of the spot,
only the wounded
man's great need.

Courage under Fire

★ ★ ★ ★ ★ ★ ★ ★ ★ ★ ★ ★ ★ ★ ★ ★ ★ ★ ★ ★

Private First Class Keith Rodriguez gripped his M-16 rifle tighter. He heard nothing but the roar of the engine and chopping of the CH-53 "Super Jolly Green Giant's" whirring rotor blades. It was just like dozens of training exercises he had been on, yet it was nothing like those flights. This was no training exercise. This was a real mission.

Fresh out of boot camp, this would be twenty-year-old Rodriguez's first combat mission. A jumble of conflicting thoughts and emotions fought for his attention. Did he want to be here, or didn't he? This was the culmination of all he had trained for. When the United States had pulled out two weeks earlier and highland had fallen to adversary the war had been officially declared over. That meant PFC Rodriguez would never have to fight in the conflict.

He remembered feeling an immediate sense of relief, but he had also felt oddly disappointed. After all the months of training, what sort of soldier would he have made? Would he have frozen in fear? Or would he have had the stuff of heroes—courage and grace under fire?

Now it looked as if Rodriguez would find out. The SS *Mayaguez,* a merchant vessel sailing under the American flag, had been boarded and captured by the adversary. Its crew had been removed from the ship and whisked away to a secret location. Rodriguez and nineteen fellow marines, two navy medics, and the chopper's air force crew were on their way to that location to rescue the crew of the *Mayaguez* in a daring surprise raid.

Eight choppers loaded with men and weapons were to take part in the mission. Intelligence indicated that the island was not well fortified or defended—they expected to encounter no more than twenty to forty enemy soldiers. The marines would greatly outnumber the adversary fighters, and resistance was expected to be light. Still, Rodriguez had an uneasy feeling. His mouth was dry, his palms sweaty no matter how many times he wiped them on his standard-issue life jacket. *Just nerves,* he told himself. *It's completely normal. Nothing will go wrong. Please, God, help nothing to go wrong,* he prayed.

The trip lasted an eternity, and it was over all too soon. Rodriguez looked at his watch as they began their sunrise descent onto the east side of the island. It was just a few minutes after 0600. *Protect me, God,* Rodriguez prayed silently. *Give me courage.* He could feel his muscles grow taut in anticipation of disembarking from the safety of the chopper and heading up that exposed beach to the cover of the jungle.

Rodriguez never got that chance. Without warning, the mission spun out of control. A hail of antiaircraft mortar rounds pierced the belly of the chopper before it could land. The CH-53 pulled up and turned back sharply, its air force crew struggling valiantly to save the chopper and those it carried. Men and weapons tumbled helplessly inside the belly of the wounded giant. Stoic marines cried out in shock and pain. Blood exploded from a handful of bullet wounds from the initial volley. Other men were hurt when they were thrown against the side of the helicopter in its violent maneuverings. Some were injured when they were hit by flying bodies and weapons.

Then there was another massive shudder accompanied by the horrible sound of an explosion. Flames quickly engulfed the helicopter as it stalled and plunged downward in a crash landing. But this was not land. Stunned and terrified, Rodriguez was overcome suddenly by a rush of seawater. Instinctively he spat out the water, but he inhaled just enough to leave him choking and gasping for air. The air he drew into his irritated lungs was filled with smoke. It was dark inside, so dark. The bumping and roiling of the chopper had turned Rodriguez's sense of direction upside down. He had no idea which direction, if any, would lead to escape.

Utter confusion and terror reigned inside the chopper.The men could hear more machine-gun fire outside. The water was rising. The smoke was growing thicker. They could hear the flames raging ever closer and feel the approaching heat. Even the seawater was growing warmer. Rodriguez looked around. Surely one of them would know what to do. But no one stepped forward. Any action, any direction, seemed as deadly as any other.

Suddenly a lone figure broke through the flame and smoke into the belly of the chopper. It was an air force staff sergeant, one of the CH-53's crew. He held his arm across his face to shield it from the flames and smoke, but he dropped it long enough to shout to the men: "You've got to get out of here now! This way. Follow me."

A thrill of relief and gratitude overwhelmed Rodriguez. Finally a direction, instructions. A way out. Those who were not dead or mortally wounded were glad to follow this man who had risked flames and water for their sake. *What sort of man is this?* Rodriguez wondered as he noted that not even a bullet wound through the leg had stopped this man from coming to the aid of the privates and lance corporals in the back.

Rodriguez could feel his skin burning and his hair

singeing as he broke through the wall of fire to the blown-open front of the chopper. As soon as he felt the heat diminish and sensed sunlight through his tightly closed eyelids, he gulped a huge breath of air. It was still smoky, but he could also smell and taste the sea and the island air. *Thank You, God!* Rodriguez prayed with great feeling.

Then reality struck him again. The staff sergeant pushed him off of the burning chopper into the water. "Stay down," he commanded. "We're under fire from the beach. Our only hope is to swim out to sea beyond range of their weapons. Swim, boys, swim for your lives. They'll come for us soon! "

His heart pounding, his lungs burning, his left arm aching from some undetermined injury, Rodriguez was happy to comply. Along with half a dozen other mobile marines, he swam with all his might. But he paused for a moment in the shadow of the dying helicopter, protected from bullets by its hulking, burning frame. His fear was momentarily superseded by admiration and awe for the courageous hero who had led the marines safely from the burning wreckage.

The man was air force. He had probably never even met any of the young marines or navy medics he had saved. Yet his heroism didn't end there. Rodriguez saw him disappear into the burning chopper one more time, emerge with more wounded marines and an M-16 rifle, then lay down covering fire to protect the retreat of the dazed and injured men. He stood his ground until he had exhausted all the ammunition, then plunged into the surf to head to sea.

Rodriguez knew he had to swim out to sea, but the water scared him almost as much as the attack from the beach. He imagined himself being pulled far out to sea, out of sight of the rescue choppers. There was a lot of blood in the water,and he knew there were sharks. He mused that being shot would be preferable to being torn and eaten.

As he clung to the chopper, working up his strength and courage for the swim, he noticed that the staff sergeant had picked up a wounded marine struggling to stay afloat and was swimming toward Rodriguez.

Suddenly Rodriguez heard a pained, fearful cry for help. It was coming from the other side of the chopper—

the side dangerously exposed to sniper fire. The staff sergeant heard it too and resolutely altered his course toward it. The first wounded marine clung to his rescuer's webbing, slowing his progress.

Rodriguez shifted to where he could see the source of the cries for help. It was a badly wounded marine. He was burned and in great pain. But perhaps his greatest fear stemmed from the fact that he had been blinded. He couldn't see danger or the way to safety. The tumultuous world of blackness and sounds had rooted him in fear to his dangerous spot.

But the sergeant didn't seem to notice the danger of the spot, only the wounded man's great need. As he stood up to reach out to the man, he was hit hard by enemy fire. One round slammed into his helmet, knocking him momentarily senseless. Additional rounds ripped away most of his life jacket but amazingly missed his body. Shaking his head clear to recover, the man grabbed the blinded marine and launched himself toward deeper water. With almost no assistance from his life preserver or from either injured man, the sergeant steadfastly made his way out to sea.

The man's commitment never wavered, but his strength did. Suddenly the sergeant's heroism gripped Rodriguez's heart. Heedless of the personal danger, he swam alongside the struggling trio. His own life preserver was intact, and he selflessly offered it—along with his assistance—to the wounded hero and his charges.

Aching muscles and tortured lungs later, they were finally out of range of the snipers. A ragged band of just thirteen men bobbed up and down on the waves; thirteen others had been lost.

The men were silent—numb—as they waited three hours for their rescuers, but Rodriguez saw many pain-filled eyes look with respect and gratitude toward the courageous staff sergeant who had saved their lives.

Rodriguez's mind was an overwhelming jumble of conflicting thoughts and feelings. But standing out among them was a sense of satisfaction and pride. He had been privileged to see true bravery and heroism. Even more important, this hero had inspired those actions in himself. Now he knew what he was made of. He would face whatever life would throw at him with grace and courage.

勇气在战火中锤炼

一等兵基思·罗德里格兹把他的M-16步枪握得更紧了。除了发动机的轰鸣声和CH-53"超级欢乐绿巨人号"的螺旋桨高速旋转产生的阵阵声浪外,他什么都听不到。这次与他以前无数次的训练科目一样,然而这次飞行与以前那些截然不同。这不是什么训练科目。这是真正的任务。

刚刚走出新兵营,这将是刚20岁的罗德里格兹的第一次战斗任务。一大堆矛盾的思绪和感情争着吸引他的注意力。他想还是不想来这呢? 这是他曾经接受的所有训练的最终目标。早在两周前,当美军撤离，高地已经陷入对方之手时，战争已经正式宣告结束。那就是说一等兵罗德里格兹再也不用在战场上战斗了。

他仍记得自己立刻有一种如释重负的感觉，不过他也感觉到多少有点失望。究竟，经过好几个月的训练，他会是哪种类型的士兵呢？他会害怕得动弹不得吗？或者他是否具有英雄的潜质——战火中的勇气和尊严？

现在，看起来罗德里格兹会找出答案的。一艘挂着美国国旗的商船"桑麻亚格斯"号被对方军队强行登船并俘虏。全体船员被驱离这艘船并被秘密转移到一个隐秘地点。罗德里格兹与19名海军陆战队队友，2名海军军医以及直升机上的空军机组人员正赶往那个地点去救援受到疯狂突袭的"桑麻亚格斯"号上的船员。

8架满载士兵和武器弹药的直升机参加了这次行动。情报说这个岛没有坚固的防御工事或防守——他们预计遭遇到的敌军不会超过40个。陆战队员的数量会远远超过对方士兵,并且估计抵抗力很弱。不管怎样,罗德里格兹仍感到一种不安。他口干舌燥,无论他怎样不断地在他笔挺的军装上衣上擦手,手掌总是有汗水。"只是紧张而已,"他对自己说,"这非常正常。不会出任何问题的。拜托,上帝,帮帮忙千万别出任何差错,"他默念道。

前行好像永远在继续,而结束得却又太快。拂晓时分,当他们开始在岛的东侧下降时, 罗德里格兹看了看表,6点刚过几分钟。"保护我,上帝,"罗德里格兹默默地祷告着。"给我勇气。"预感到即将要离开直升机的庇护,跨越无遮拦的海滩冲向茂密的丛林,他能感觉得到全身的肌肉绷得紧紧的。

罗德里格兹永远不会有那样的机会了。没有任何警报,整个团队立刻处于失控状态。飞机还没有来得及着陆,一排防空迫击炮弹就射穿了直升机的腹部。CH–53向上拉升并急速回转,机上的空军机组人员竭尽全力英勇地挽救着飞机以及机上所载的东西。人和武器在受伤的大家伙的机舱里无助地上下翻飞。坚强的陆战队员在惊恐和疼痛中大声呼喊着。在刚才的枪炮齐射中,几个受了枪伤的伤员的伤口鲜血迸溅出来。强烈的飞机操控过程中,有几个人被甩到直升机的机舱侧面而受了伤。还有一些人被飞舞的身体和武器装备击伤。

一声可怕的爆炸声,紧接着就是一个巨大的震颤。随着直升机熄火,飞机急速向下猛冲坠毁,火焰迅速吞没了直升机。然而这里不是陆地。惊恐之中,罗德里格兹突然呛了一口海水。他本能地吐出口里的水,但是他吸入的空气只够让他不会窒息供给喘气用。他吸入受刺激的肺里的空气中全是烟。烟雾里一片漆黑。直升机的撞击和骚乱已经让罗德里格兹的方向感颠三倒四。他不知道该往哪个方向,如果有可能的话,逃生。

直升机里一片狼藉,异常恐怖。大家能听到外面有更多的机枪射击的声音。水在上涨,烟越来越浓。他们听得到火焰怒吼着蔓延,离他们越来越近,并且可以感受得到正在逼近的热量。甚至连海水也逐渐热起来。罗德里格兹看了一下四周,他们中肯定会有人知道该做些什么。但是没人向前迈步。任何举动,任何指示似乎都一样是致命的。

突然,一个孤独的身影冲破火焰和烟雾闯进机舱内。他是CH-53机组人员之一,是一名空军士官参谋。他抬起手臂交叉在脸的前面遮挡火和烟。此刻他边放下手臂边向这些人喊:"你们现在必须离开这儿!这边来,跟着我。"

一股解脱和感激的兴奋之情涌上罗德里格兹的心头。最终有了方向,确切地说有了指示—— 一条出去的路。那些还活着的或者受伤的士兵很乐意跟着这个为了他们而冒生命危险越火涉水的人。"这是个什么样的人呢?"罗德里格兹疑惑着。因为他注意到这个人的腿上有不止一处的枪伤让他可以不用帮助这些落在后面的士兵和下士。

罗德里格兹冲过火墙向炸坏了的直升机前部移动时,他感到皮肤烧着了,头发也烧焦了。当感到热度降低,他透过紧闭的眼皮察觉到阳光时,也大大地喘了口气。天空仍是烟雾弥漫,不过他可以闻得到品得出大海和海岛的气息。"感谢上帝!"罗德里格兹怀着深深的感情祈祷着。

然而现实又把他拉了回来。这位士官参谋把他推离燃烧的直升机直到水里。"压低身体,"他命令道,"我们处于来自对面海滩的攻击之中。我们唯一的希望就是向海里游,游出他们的武器射程范围。游啊,小伙子们,为了你们的生命游啊。他们一会儿就会来抓我们的!"

罗德里格兹的心怦怦直跳,肺里冒火,左手臂不知被什么伤得很痛,他愿意听从这个人的命令。身边还有6名能动的陆战队员和他一起拼命地游着。但是,他在熊熊燃烧的、即将消失的直升机残骸的阴影里逗留了片刻,靠飞机巨大的骨架作掩护挡子弹。瞬间,他的恐惧被他对这位英勇英雄的崇拜和敬畏所取代,是这个英雄带领着陆战队员们安全地撤离这具熊熊燃烧的残骸。

　　这个人是名空军。大概,他甚至以前从未碰到过任何一个他所拯救的这些年轻的陆战队员或者海军军医。然而,他的英雄壮举远未就此结束。罗德里格兹看见他再次消失在燃烧的直升机里,又钻出来,身边带着伤势更重的陆战队员和M-16步枪,然后伏下身火力掩护昏迷和受伤的人撤退。他在原地坚持到耗完所有的弹药,然后跳入浪中朝大海前进。

　　罗德里格兹清楚,自己得朝大海的方向游,但是海水几乎和来自岸上的攻击一样让他恐惧。他想象着自己被拉到大海里很远的距离,看不见救援的直升机的情形。水里有很多血。他知道水里有鲨鱼 。他想与其被撕碎吃掉还不如被枪打死。

　　当他贴着飞机残骸,积蓄力量和勇气要游泳时,他注意到那个士官参谋搀起一名受伤的陆战队员拼命地保持飘浮姿势,正朝着罗德里格兹这边游。

　　突然,罗德里格兹听到一声痛苦可怕的求救声,声音来自于直升机的另一侧,那一侧暴露在狙击步枪的射程之内,极其危险。士官参谋也听到了，毅然地改变行动方向朝声音的方向移动。起先的那个伤员紧贴着他的救护者的腰带，这减缓了士官的行动。

罗德里格兹转移到他能看得到的发出求救声源的地方。那是个伤势严重的陆战队员。他被烧伤了，疼痛难忍。不过也许他最大的恐惧源自于他已经变成瞎子的事实。他看不见危险或者安全的出路。黑暗和喧闹混杂的骚乱世界早已将内心惊恐万分的他置于危险的境地。

但是，这位士官好像没有注意到现场的危险。眼里只有受伤者的迫切需要。当他起身伸出手去够那个人时，敌人的子弹结结实实地击中了他。一颗弹头砰的一声击中他的头盔，打得他短暂地不省人事。许多子弹把他的防弹衣撕烂了，但是都出人意料地没打中身体。这人抖了抖脑袋让自己恢复清醒，迅速抓住失明的陆战队员，冲刺般朝深水区游去。在几乎没有得到任何防护装备保护或者伤员帮助的情况下，这个士官坚定地朝着大海前进。

这人的行为从未动摇过,但他已经体力不支了。突然间,士官的英勇行为震撼了罗德里格兹的心。他不顾个人安危与正在挣扎的3个人肩并肩游水。他自己的防弹衣完好无损,于是他无私地把它给了受伤的英雄和伤员以尽他的绵薄之力。

经过一阵肌肉酸痛和肺部难耐痛苦之后,他们最终走出了狙击手的视野。13个衣衫褴褛的人在海浪上浮浮沉沉;另外13个人牺牲了。

这些人默默地、有些麻木地等待着救援,等了3个小时之久。但是,罗德里格兹看见许多双充满痛苦的眼睛都看着挽救了他们生命的英勇的士官参谋,眼神里带着崇敬和感激。

罗德里格兹的大脑里无序地充斥着各种各样的想法和感情,但是站在他们中间就有一种满足和自豪的感觉。他有幸亲眼目睹了真正的勇敢行为和英雄壮举,更重要的是这位英雄激励了他自己的壮举。现在他明白了自己是什么样子的人了。未来,他将用尊严和勇气面对人生丢给他的一切考验。

Heroes
Take
Notice

Chapter
7

英雄体察入微

Your lifestyle of selfless service to others is making you great in My eyes! A good life and deeds done in humility showcase your wisdom and understanding. As you humble yourself, I'm promoting you.

你无私奉献他人的生活方式使得你在我的眼里变得越来越伟大！美好的生活和谦恭的行为举止揭示了你的智慧和善解人意。当你变得谦逊时，我正在奖励你。

I'll reward your actions as you serve others as if you're serving Me. And as you continue to give, I'll generously bless you with much more than you invested.

CHEERING YOU ON TO LOVE AND GOOD DEEDS,
YOUR SERVANT JESUS
—from Mark 10:43–45; James 3:13, 4:10;
Ephesians 6:7–8; Luke 6:38

我将答谢你的行为，因你服务他人就像你在为我尽职一样。在你不断地付出之时,我会慷慨地回馈给你远远超出你所付出的一切。

为你付出爱和善举喝彩
你的仆人耶稣
——摘自《马可福音》10:43;《雅各书 》3:13,4:10;
《以弗所书》6:7-8;《路加福音》6:38

Some people can pass by others in need and never even see them. The masses rush past without pausing to notice or taking time to care. It's as though they don't exist.

But heroes stop and take notice. They see the unpopular, unappreciated, sometimes unlovely people around us. Heroes find needs and meet them, understand hurts and heal them.

Heroes aren't concerned with rewards or recognition. Instead of wanting to be seen, they see others through a singular scope of clarity. Heroes know that hurting people are not statistics but individuals who need love and care.

Are you a hero? Take notice today of the people you normally pass without a thought. How many of them are lonely or sad or in need? What can you do to help? You don't have to fix every problem. Heroes rarely help everyone.   What distinguishes heroes from the crowd is the willingness to notice what others choose to ignore—individual souls, who are valuable and who just might need a hero today.

有些人可能不会过问需要帮助的人,甚

至连看都不看他们。大多数人匆匆走过,不会停下来

去注意或者花时间去关心一下他们,好像他们根本不存

在一样。

但是英雄们会止步并给予关注。他们关注着我们周

围那些不受欢迎的人,不识时务的人,有时是那些令

人讨厌的人。英雄发现并满足他们的需要,英雄

体察并治愈他们的伤痛。

英雄不关心回报或者出名。相

反,因为不想让人发现,他们

通过一种单一而清

晰的视角观

察别人。英雄懂得,受伤害的人不是统

计学上的数字而是那些需要关爱和照顾的单个的人。

　　你是英雄吗?现在起,不要犹豫,去观察往常与你匆

匆走过的人。他们中有多少人孤苦无依,有多少人满怀伤

感,又有多少人需要帮助呢?你能做点什么去帮助他们

呢?你不需要解决所有问题。英雄不可能帮助所有

人。将英雄与普通人群区别开来的东西就是他

们愿意去观察别人选择忽略的东西——

个人的心灵,有些人的心灵很珍

贵,还有些人的心灵可能恰

好正需要一位英雄

拯救。

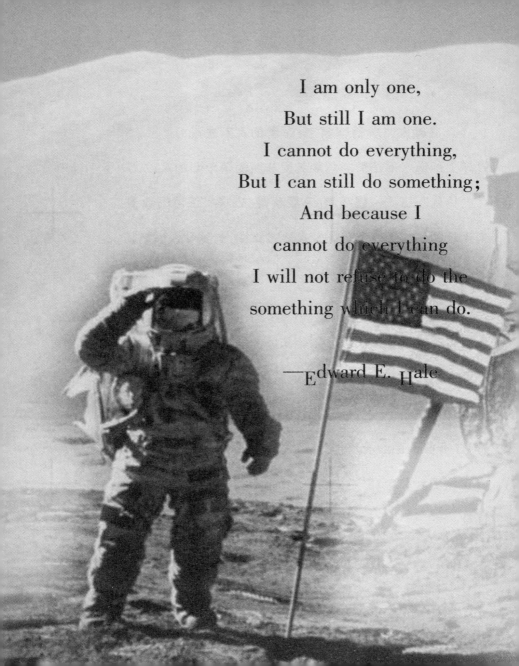

I am only one,
But still I am one.
I cannot do everything,
But I can still do something;
And because I
cannot do everything
I will not refuse to do the
something which I can do.

—Edward E. Hale

我只是一个人，

但是不管怎样我仍旧是个人，

我不可能做所有的事，

但我仍可以做些事情；

正因为我不可能做所有的事，

我才不会拒绝做我能做的事。

——爱德华·伊·霍尔

那天晚上，麦根将喜爱的毯子紧紧地围在身上，紧紧蜷缩其中。突然她坐起来，"就这么办！"

That *night Megan* *snuggled* up *in her favorite blanket,* *wrapping it around her tightly. Suddenly* she sat up. "*That's it!* "

A Blanket Statement

★ ★

Megan's excitement grew by the minute as she brushed her hair in preparation for her biggest date of the year. Two or three times a month, twelve-year-old Megan and her dad, Ted, would have a "date"—a special father-daughter outing. Sometimes they went to see a movie, other times to a favorite restaurant or ice cream parlor. But Megan's favorite kind of outing was shopping.

Shopping took half a day. Megan got to visit all her favorite stores in the mall, and her dad would let her try on outfit after outfit as he patiently waited for her ongoing fashion show. But today was special—her favorite shopping trip of the year. This was their Christmas shopping trip. Instead of going to the nearby mall, Megan and her father would take the subway into the city. Megan loved the elaborate Christmas decorations and the huge department stores. She was mesmerized by one massive floor-to-ceiling tree loaded with twinkling lights and sparkling ornaments.

Megan had saved her baby-sitting money and allowance to buy gifts for her family. Then, after shopping all afternoon, she and her dad would eat at a classic downtown diner, go to an early Christmas movie, and ride the subway back home laden with gifts and priceless memories.

Everything was just as fun and festive as Megan had anticipated. But the stores were so crowded and the prices so high that she only found a few gifts that she both liked and could afford. *No matter,* she thought. *In a few days, I'll just go with Mom to some local stores for the rest of the gifts.* The experience of Christmastime downtown was worth the crowded bustle. She still had most of her money to find some really nice presents later. So Megan and her dad set off for their favorite diner and enthusiastically ate huge, juicy burgers while they deliberated over which Christmas movie to see.

Suddenly Megan glanced out the diner window and squealed. "Dad, look! This is just perfect. It's beginning to snow! " Light, powdery flakes drifted lazily and began coating the city in a magical white Christmas blanket. Megan was glad they had checked the weather forecast and dressed warmly,as the temperature had dropped swiftly into the low twenties.

As Megan hung on to her dad with one hand and carried two shopping bags in the other, the two raced out of the diner and down the four blocks toward the theater. Warm air from the subway below rose up through the grates in the sidewalks and formed clouds of steam as it hit the cold, wintry air. Megan was enjoying the city sights when she felt her right foot bump something and heard a moan escape from a formless heap.

Startled, Megan stopped and tugged her dad back to the creature she had kicked. Lying bundled in a tattered coat and covered with newspapers was one of the city's many homeless people who found some small warmth by sleeping on the subway grates when the nights grew cold.

"I'm sorry to have kicked you, sir," Megan apologized.

"Don't worry about him," her dad said as he nudged her away. "Let's move on and not disturb him." The man simply moaned again and turned over, ignoring them.

Megan took her dad's hand, and they moved on toward the theater. But the show that night failed to capture Megan's attention. All she could think about was the shivering, homeless man with nothing to shelter him but a few newspapers.

"You're awfully quiet," Ted commented as they headed home on the subway. "Still thinking about that homeless man we stumbled onto?" he asked.

Tears welled up in Megan's eyes. "Dad, isn't there anything we can do to help? After all, it's Christmas, and it's really cold."

"What do you suggest?" Ted asked. Megan thought hard all the way home, but the situation seemed hopeless. What could a twelve-year-old do about the city's homeless population?

When Megan and her dad arrived home, her mom and brother greeted them cheerfully and asked about their excursion, but the father and daughter were subdued. They relayed what had happened, but no one seemed hopeful that anything could be done to help the situation.

That night Megan snuggled up in her favorite blanket, wrapping it around herself tightly. Suddenly she sat up. *"That's it!"* she thought. Jumping out of bed, she snatched the blanket and ran into the family room where her mom and dad were watching television.

"Dad! Mom! I know what we can do! " Megan exclaimed. "Let's get all of our blankets together and give them to those homeless people. At least they'll be warmer on the cold nights! "

Megan's parents gave several reasons why handing out a few blankets wouldn't do much good and explained that it could be dangerous. But Megan persisted. She collected the rest of her Christmas money and vowed to buy more blankets with it. As she argued her case, the late-night local news forecasted single-digit temperatures and at least twelve inches of snow by morning. "We've got to go back tonight," Megan pleaded. "Some of those people could freeze without our blankets."

Something about Megan's innocent yet convicting plea touched her parents' hearts. Though they knew it was impractical, they gave in and gathered all the blankets they could find. Most stores were closed at that hour, but the family stopped at a local Wal-Mart so Megan could purchase a few more blankets.

The travelers were quite a sight—a middle-class, suburban family of four, carrying a dozen blankets on an hour long, late-night subway trip to the inner city. When they finally arrived at the stop near the theater, Megan raced to the top of the stairs toward the grate. The man was still there, trying to sleep and huddling for warmth with another man who had crowded in on his grate. Megan's family caught up with her just as she covered the first man with her blanket and reached for another for the second man.

Two blankets distributed, ten to go. Megan saw two more men covered with cardboard boxes and sleeping against a building. As she approached, one of the men jumped up, cursed the family, and took off down the street with his box in hand. The other man didn't move, and Megan wasn't about to be deterred. She fearlessly covered the other sleeping transient with a blanket while her dad stood guard.

Nine more blankets left to give away. Turning back toward the street, they were surprised to come face to face with two police officers. "What are you doing?" One of them demanded to know. "You could get yourselves mugged out here like this! "

Ted patiently explained what they were doing while the second officer went to the patrol car to give a report. "I don't think this is such a safe idea," the first officer cautioned.

"But they could freeze without the blankets! " Megan pleaded tearfully. "I've spent all of my Christmas money on these new blankets. I have to give them away before it's too late for someone." Touched by the girl's compassion and determination, the officers decided to follow a few paces behind the family as an informal escort for their mission of mercy.

Unknown to any of them, a local television news team in a remote broadcast van had picked up the unusual police report on their scanner. Now they pulled alongside the curb just as the young hero found another homeless man sleeping on a subway grate and carefully covered him with a blanket.

The news team recorded the young girl's crusade to make a small but important difference for a few homeless people. When interviewed, Megan told of the need for homeless people to have blankets on such a cold night.

Early the next morning, Megan's mission was broadcast on the local news. A network morning show also aired a brief segment on Megan's efforts, and her plea struck a nerve in the national audience. Calls flooded in, and overnight, TV stations became the depositories for people donating blankets for the homeless. Local street missions and homeless shelters also picked up the crusade.

Over the next week, Megan's plea was rebroadcast again and again. Her one-person crusade launched a movement throughout her city and in other urban areas to provide blankets and aid to the homeless. Thousands of them received blankets, food, and shelter during that icy Christmas season...all because one girl took notice and refused to ignore another person's need.

圣诞夜的毯子

麦根梳着头发为今年她最盛大的约会做准备。她的兴奋之情随着时间一分一秒过去变得越来越强烈。12岁的麦根和她的爸爸泰德每个月会有两三次的约会，这个"约会"是个有着特别意义的父女俩的户外活动。有时他们会去看一场电影，去喜欢的餐馆或冰激凌店。但是麦根最喜欢的户外活动是逛街购物。

逛街要花半天时间。麦根可以光顾这个小地方她喜欢的所有店铺，她的爸爸会让她一件一件地试衣服，而他则耐心地等待着欣赏她表演的流行服装秀。不过，今天很特别——这会是她今年最喜

拥抱·爱——勇敢的心

欢的购物之旅。这次外出是他们的圣诞购物之旅。麦根和她的父亲不是去附近的购物中心，而是乘地铁进城。麦根喜爱那些精巧的圣诞装饰以及巨大的商场。一棵一房多高挂满闪灯和耀眼夺目装饰品的大树让她着迷。

麦根早就把她帮别人看小孩挣的钱和零用钱攒起来要给家人买礼物了。到时候，逛完街就是下午了，她和她父亲将要到闹市区一家古典的餐厅用餐，接着去看一部圣诞开场电影，最后乘地铁满载礼物和无尽的美好回忆回家。

一切都和麦根当初设想的一样快乐有趣。不过，人多太挤，商品太贵，到最后她只找到很少几件既喜欢又买得起的礼物。"没关系，"她想，"过几天，我会和妈妈一起去当地的一些店铺买其余的礼物。"圣诞期间闹市区的体验价值在于拥挤和喧闹。过一会儿，她手里还有许多钱用来寻找一些真正好看的礼物。于是麦根和爸爸开始出发去他们喜爱的餐厅，然后一边疯狂地大吃特吃又大又多汁的汉堡，一边寻思着去看哪部圣诞电影。

突然，麦根往餐厅的窗户外面看了一眼，随即尖叫道："爸爸，快看！真是太棒了。开始下雪了！"轻而薄，如粉状的雪花懒洋洋地飘落下来，开始给城市披上一层梦幻般的白色圣诞外装。麦根庆幸他们早就查过天气预报并且穿得暖暖地，这时的气温已经骤降到零下20多度。

麦根紧紧握住爸爸的手，用另一只手拎着两个购物袋，两个人跑出餐厅，穿过4个街区走向剧院。热气从地道里冒出来，穿过人行道上的铁栅栏，当遭遇到冰冷的空气时形成了蒸汽云雾。麦根正欣赏着城市景色，突然觉得右脚踩住了什么东西，同时听到一声哀号从一堆不规则的物体中发出来。

麦根吃了一惊，停下脚步把她的爸爸拽回到她刚刚踢到的那堆东西前。一个人躺在那里，衣衫破烂不堪，盖着几张报纸。他是这个城市里许多无家可归的人中的一个；他们在夜晚越来越冷的时候就寻找某个微弱的热源睡在地道的壁炉旁。

"很抱歉,先生,我踢到你了。"麦根道歉说。

"不用管他,"她的爸爸边说边推着她离开。"我们接着走吧,别打扰他。"那个人仅仅又哼了一声就转过身去,不理他们了。

麦根抓住她爸爸的手,他们继续朝剧院走。但是,那晚的电影没能抓住麦根的注意力。她满脑子都在想着那个浑身发抖,无家可归的人——他除了几张报纸外没有任何的御寒之物。

"你太安静了,"在他们乘地铁回家的路上,泰德评论道,"还在想我们绊到的那个无家可归的人吗?"他问道。

麦根眼里满含泪水。"爸爸,难道就没有我们可以做的事情去帮助他吗?毕竟,今天是圣诞节,而且天真的很冷。"

"你有什么建议呢?"泰德问。麦根回家的路上都努力在想,但是情况似乎是解决无望。一个12岁的小姑娘又能对这个城市的流浪汉做些什么呢?

麦根和她爸爸回到家时,她的妈妈和哥哥高兴地欢迎她并询问有关他们远足的情况,但是父女俩都支支吾吾。他们轮流讲述着发生的一切,但是似乎没有一个人对做点什么去解决这种情况抱希望。

那天晚上,麦根将喜爱的毯子紧紧地围在自己身上,紧紧蜷缩其中。突然她坐起来。"就这么办!"她想道,她跳下床,抓起毯子跑进客厅里,她的爸爸和妈妈正在那看电视。

"爸爸!妈妈!我知道我们可以做什么了!"麦根叫喊道。"我们把我们所有的毯子集中在一起然后把毯子发给那些无家可归的人。至少在这样冷的夜晚,他们会暖和一点!"

麦根的父母列举了好几个将毯子分发出去不会有太大作用的原因,并解释说那样做会有危险。但是麦根仍坚持己见。她把她剩下的圣诞要花的钱集中起来并发誓要用这些钱来多买几条毯子。正当她提出自己的观点时,当地晚间新闻预报说气温骤降并且到明天早晨,雪至少会有12英尺厚。"我们必须今晚就回去,"麦根请求说,"没有我们的毯子,他们中的某些人可能会冻僵的。"

麦根的天真无邪,更是坚定的恳求打动了她父母的心。虽然他们清楚那是不切实际的行为,但是他们让步了,然后将所有能找得到的毯子集中在一起。大部分的店铺当时都关门了,但是这家人在当地一家沃尔玛超市停下来,这样的话麦根就能多买几条毯子。

这一行人真是一道风景—— 一个中产阶级,住在郊区的四口之家,抱着12条毯子坐了长达一个小时的深夜地铁前往市中心。当他们最终到达位于剧院附近的地铁站时,麦根就冲向楼梯顶向壁炉旁跑去。那个人还在那里,他和另外一个挤进他这个壁炉的人抱成一团互相取暖正要睡觉。麦根的家人赶上她,这时她正在给第一个人盖毯子,然后伸手拿另一条毯子给第二个人盖上。

两条毯子分出去了,还有10条要发。麦根看见两三个人,身上盖着纸箱子正靠着一幢建筑物在睡觉。当她走上前去时,其中一个人跳起来,骂这一家人,然后手里拿着纸箱顺着街道跑了,其他人没有动。麦根不想拖延。她毫不害怕地替其他熟睡的过客盖上一条毯子，同时她的爸爸就在旁边守护着她。

还有9条毯子要分发出去。他们转过身面朝街道，他们正好与两名警察面对面相遇，彼此都很惊讶。"你们在干什么？"其中一个查问道，"像这样在这儿你们会被抢劫的！"

泰德耐心地解释着他们所做的事，同时第二个警察走向巡逻车去报告情况。"我想这是个不太安全的主意，"第一个警官告诫说。

"可是没有毯子他们可能会冻僵的！" 麦根泪眼婆娑地恳求道。"我已经把我所有的过圣诞节的钱都用来买这些新毯子了。对某些人来说在情况还没有太糟之前，我得把毯子发出去。"出于对女孩的仁慈之心和毅力的感动，警官决定跟随一家人之后几步远作为对她仁慈之举的一种非正式保护。

他们谁都不知道，在一部视讯遥控广播车里，当地一家电视新闻采编组工作人员早已通过他们的雷达接受到警察汇报的这一不寻常事件。现在，他们把车停在围栏边上，这时小英雄发现另一个流浪者正睡在一个地铁壁炉旁，然后她小心地为他盖上一条毯子。

这个新闻小组记录下这个小姑娘的圣举，她对这几个无家可归的人来说创造了很小但是却很重要的差异。当被采访时，麦根讲述说，在那么冷的夜晚无家可归的人身上需要有毯子盖。

第二天清早，麦根的行为在当地新闻中播出。一个早间网络节目也就麦根的努力行为广播了一小段。她的祈求震动了这个国家观众的神经。电话如潮水般涌进来，一夜之间，电视台成了人们为无家可归的人捐毯子的储物室。当地街道代表和流浪汉收容所也积极行动起来。

在接下来的一周里，麦根的恳求被一遍一遍地广播。她一个人的圣举引发了一场遍及她所在的城市以及其他城市向无家可归的人捐献毯子和提供帮助的运动。成千上万的流浪汉在那个冰冷的圣诞季节收到了毯子、食品以及居所……全都是因为一个小女孩观察入微并拒绝忽视他人的需要啊！

Journal

★ ★ ★ ★ ★ ★ ★ ★

Write your own story of a hero who has "hugged" your life and deserves to be celebrated.   Then share your story with your hero to express your heartfelt thanks.

_____

_____

_____

_____

_____

_____

_____

_____

_____

_____

_____

_____

_____

_____

日　志

★ ★ ★ ★ ★ ★ ★ ★

　　写下你自己的一个关于一位英雄"拥抱"过你的生命并且应该得到颂扬的故事。然后同你心中的英雄一起分享你的故事，以此来表达你对他或她的衷心谢意。

_____

_____

_____

_____

_____

_____

_____

_____

_____

_____

_____

_____

_____

_____

_____

_____

_____

_____

_____

_____

_____

_____

_____

_____

_____

_____

_____

_____

_____

_____

_____

_____

_____

_____

_____

_____

_____

_____

_____

_____

_____

_____

_____

_____